Cover art by Lawrence Boffa

STORY AVE

PETE KEARNEY

COPYRIGHT © 2016 PETE KEARNEY

ISBN: 9781942500308

Boulevard Books

The New Face of Publishing

www.BoulevardBooks.org

TABLE OF CONTENTS

EVERYTHNG IN ONE DAY   P. 4

LINGAS TO CARLISLE   P.83

Everything in One Day

In appreciation

Steve Katz

Jim Gibbons has been a thorn in my side since night school. I remember meeting him at a Queens College creative writing class. Our assignment was to go through our short stories and cross out any clichés we may have used. He comes over to me. I don't know him from Adam.

"Learning to write in a creative writing class is like learning to play baseball by trading baseball cards," he says.

I stand to shake his hand. "Aren't you the instructor?"

Then there's the Queens College Writing Contest. I won first prize. It was over thirty years ago. Days go by without me mentioning it.

I wrote a book about a toaster that loads four slices of bread, before turning on a spit. When the openings go from vertical to horizontal it ejects toast - buttered and sliced. This won first prize. It was just my good luck. That year the judges loved toast.

I grab my $1,000 prize and run to Gibbons's apartment. At his front door I'm dancing around, waving the check like I'm drying the ink on it. He doesn't ask me in.

"What are you going to do now – beat up some cub scouts?"

You know that face he makes. He's diminishing my award and the quality of the competition. He's jealous and I know why. He had his own entry in the contest; a play, a play about a waffle iron. Come on.

We played handball as partners back then. It wasn't until 1991 that we recognized that being opponents was more fun than being teammates. It's more pleasurable to ruin the day of a guy who hangs out with you afterwards.

In order to establish a clear record of supremacy, a league was formed. Whoever leads after eleven seasons is victor emeritus. We envisioned a campaign protracted as the Vietnam War. The exercise would be healthful, I told myself. This teenage pursuit would keep me young.

This recounting retraces the contest as it unfolded in 1997. I had put aside my toaster novel and taken a job in transportation sales after not finishing college. Suspecting I was short on people skills, I took the Dale Carnegie course. It perfected my handshake and elbow cup. I started looking people in the eye until they looked away. I will repeat your name the minute I meet you and lock you in a memory cell. As a smoker regrets his first Lucky, I curse my first good year in sales. After that it was easy or impossible depending on the day. Salesmen are the left-handed relievers of the business world. If you can throw a little, someone will sign you. I didn't grow roots anywhere but I landed on my feet after every dismount. I was never without a business card.

MARCH 20

Angela gets her period on the first day of spring. It's a bad omen for the start of the handball season. I need to be free of all distraction. I want the special spring in my step that comes in the aftermath of lovemaking.

Ring generalship, the counter punch, the jab, the feint and footwork all come together in this sport that suggests an outdoor prize fight with no punches landed. I expect to be going into opening weekend flat-footed and wearing last year's sneakers.

Boxing and handball share the need for a good left hand. You're not living on a backhand in handball. Your weak side has to be your strong side. You've got to move one way and have your shadow move another. Handball is chess on a Saltine half-court.

6

Connie loved making love during her period. Connie is not with me anymore. Angela and I haven't been going out long enough for her to be comfortable making love while bleeding.

Gibbons is newly married. He's likely to be in a great frame of mind for opening day. I'm not blaming Angela. She's from the Philippines. What does she know about handball?

Angela asks, "Would you say I'm a good kisser?"

"Horrible," I say, "Picture a Ferrari fueled with lighter fluid."

She goes up on her toes to challenge my review. Her lips part and I touch a tongue cool as a mango wedge. My fear of starting the season is waylaid.

Angela is classic Filipino beauty with a black cat of hair. Her first marriage ended when he walked out with no explanation. She swears she saw no sign of it coming.

"I have no idea of what I did wrong."

"Go out with me and I'll know in two weeks."

"Just like that we're a couple?"

"You know I adore you."

"Blah blah blah.

I hurt my back at work and walk on court feeling like I'm carrying a sandbag over my left shoulder. Gibbons is stretching. It's a cold day with winds strong enough to hold a ball in bounds. I win the first game 21-16.

He gets inspired in the second game. I see him moving his serve around looking for a weakness. He's feinting then falling back, classic guerilla warfare. I'm on the backline comparing Connie's kisses with Angela's kisses. It's an unfair thing to do. For three years, Connie and I kissed up and down the alphabet in English and in French. Connie has a married woman's kiss fired by the thought she isn't kissing the man she married. Angela and I have been kissing for a couple of weeks. She kisses like a single girl, free of intrigue. Gibbons wins 21-6.

Embarrassed by that score, I give a better account of myself in the third game. I lose 21-18. My shoulder has loosened up and we're on our way to the bar. Our handball season is underway. Warmer days are evoked by a billboard for the Sports Illustrated swimsuit issue.

A single car is parked on a street. A handball sails over a fence. It rolls under the car straight as a green shot. The ball rests equidistant from the sides of the car. You have to belly crawl underneath to retrieve it. This is a law of nature dating back to the invention of the ball and the automobile. If I'm in a tent, it's raining, another sure thing.

Handball players are found at neighborhood playgrounds. They flock to the wall like primates from Kubrick's space movie. The rules of handball exist in the ether of the neighborhood you're playing in. The gods of handball are secular gods. Hindu is the god of the unexplainable bounce. Setup is the god of fatal generosity. Killer is the god who cannot be answered. Ace is the god of divine service.

8

Long Island City is back-parked into a spot between the Triborough Bridge and the Midtown Tunnel. The 59th Bridge pokes a finger in its midsection. The neighborhood is a mile wide; its western border is the East River. It is home to three access routes to Manhattan, two movie studios, and dozens of auto body shops too small to swing a dented cat in. The hood has a pizzeria on every other block.

LIC boasts a Budweiser plant, a Pepsi sign, and two Con Ed stacks whose smoke underlines the cityscape if you're landing at La Guardia. The half dozen handball courts within its boundaries serve as the dance floor for the Interboro Handball League. Loser supplies the trophy.

There is a polite slap of palms at the end of each game but no chest bumping or pats on the ass. Touching gloves is a formality in boxing not observed in handball. We don't wear gloves. It's understood you're not friends for the duration of the contest. You want to win every game. I'm a competitive guy and Gibbons is as well. He slept with my wife so I guess he's straight.

You huddle in football and basketball; in boxing you confer with your corner. You're on your own in handball. I call out the score at the beginning and end of every volley. Other than "line" "block" and "out" there's no dialogue. The soundtrack is the clap of the ball on the wall and the pop of the ball off your palm. It's summer camp ballet with a two note orchestra.

Our league exists with a minimum of equipment. A rock is used to scrape a serve line. The contestants are the ground crew kicking debris off the court. Other than Gibbons's knee brace, our only prop is a bodega rubber ball. It's mano a mano against a single wall and don't even mention paddles. At times we've played adjacent to paddleball foursomes, tame as Canasta parties. We are shirtless palookas throwing haymakers on a shade-less playground. Gibbons and I are the only two

9

members of the Interboro Handball League. Everyone else has better things to do.

We drink at McReilley's after each three game set. One of us has lost. Gibbons sulks when I prevail. I turn on him when I don't.

"At least I don't have to watch you sulk." I console myself.

"Is that your excuse?"

"I'm not a sore loser."

"You've had more practice."

MARCH 23

PALM SUNDAY

"Lord I am not worthy of your blessings. The shots I made today were remarkable. You made me look so cool. With my back to the wall, I hit the ball over my shoulder and it came down a killer. Did you see me bless myself? Why am I asking you?

I do not deserve your support. I turned my back on Connie. Angela is helping me get over her. I may appear to be consumed with my own indulgences. I plead for your intercession. Straddling relationships may compromise the handball talent you've given me. . Bear with me and accept my humble prayer Amen."

MARCH 27

Lori is a girlfriend from college.

"Have you spoken to Connie?" I ask.

"Is that the only reason you called?"

"Cut it out, please."

"I spoke to her for about an hour last night."

Lori and I were a duo at night school. I introduced her to Connie; they have bonded over a mutual impatience with me.

"Does she hate me?"

"Pretty much. You betrayed her"

I never did anything behind her back."

"Angela?"

"I told her all about Angela."

"It really hurt when you didn't show up that day."

"I didn't say I would. I said I would if I could."

"That's what I mean, bullshit. You only want what you can't have. The same crap you pulled with me."

"What about her husband?"

"He's at home recovering, the big jerk. If his wife wants to be with you, don't go off a cliff over it. How smart can she be if she likes you?""

"I'm sick," I say.

"Sure you are."

"Okay, everything is my fault."

"What about Connie?"

"I love her but under these circumstances we can't see each other."

"In the meantime, fuck anyone you want." Click.

MARCH 28

The second week of the season we are at the 36th Avenue playground on the afternoon of Good Friday. It's warm and by the second game we have our shirts off. I win 21-19. Gibbons wins the second and third game by the same score 21-16. At three o'clock I kneel on court in observance of Christ's death on the cross. Lori's hang up line plays in my head like the Mr. Softee tune.

We go to the bar and drink Bass. I tell Gibbons about Lori's phone bomb but he's not listening. He's intent on entering the scores in our logbook. I'm behind by two games.

APRIL 4

The Friday after Good Friday, I'm making my sales calls in Sunset Park. I'm after a company called Professional Product Resources. I can't get the traffic manager on the phone so I'm dropping in cold. I stroll past the NO SOLICITORS sign. A guy reading the Daily News at the front desk points me to the warehouse.

"Richie handles shipping."

I find three guys standing at the mouth of a conveyor belt.

"Richie?" One of the three turns. I reach to shake hands.

"I don't see salesmen without appointments."

"Pretend I'm invisible." I smile, my empty hand returning to the gate.

Richie is holding a masking tape dispenser. The conveyor belt is carrying down packs of the foam foot pads you put on corns. They are dropping into a shipping carton.

"Not today, Jose," he turns away from me.

"Well thanks for taking the time to say 'Hello' but my name's not Jose." I'm talking to the back of his head.

Being a salesman means taking shit from a guy whose job it is to count foot pads dropping into a box. It is inviting people with the narrowest of authorities to exercise that authority over you. I go outside and call Gibbons.

"Game time."

"I have to be somewhere at five."

"Leave now, we'll have time."

We play at 21st playground called the Cow Palace because a life-sized cow overlooks the court from the roof of a supermarket next door. Gibbons is not ready for my intensity. I lead in both games wire to wire. Then he claims he's running late. I drive him to the subway.

"Thanks for coming out on no notice."

"For the record, I don't play salesmen without an appointment." I had told him about my sales call. He's out of the car, without shaking hands.

I take Roz to her niece's bats mitzvah. Her hair is teased into a bulb as inviting to touch as attic insulation. She's in a tight low-cut dress favored by fat girls on prom night. I've worked with Roz on and off for twenty years; she's always been an unmade bed. Last year she was widowed. I'm divorced. We started going out.

Wide as she is tall, Roz keeps a smear of lipstick on her teeth. Her exuberant lilt plucks your ear hair. Every conversation is a minefield of non-sequiturs. I only graduated high school but next to her I'm Alfred Einstein.

The affair is held at the Westchester Country Club. Roz and I are the only couple without kids. I go to the bar. They are not serving alcohol. The party emcee is Mod Squad ensemble. A young Alan King is flanked by a blonde with a button nose and a black kid with a shaved head and two earrings in one ear.

The kids do the Alley Cat, Hokey Pokey, followed by the Macarena and musical chairs. I'm tapping my watch to make sure it's working. Roz walks me around introducing me to her family. These are the same people who skipped her husband's funeral. Now she's showing me off as her new goy and making cracks that suggest her and I are intimate.

The niece cuts a cake suitable for a wedding. The kids are wild with loud music, snacks and soda. I take Roz back to my apartment so I can get out of my suit. The party had closed with everyone linking arms and singing "Keep Shining".

"Do you have a date tonight?" she asks.

"I'm not staying home."

"Oh, so you're going to see Angela." She picks at the bedspread she's sitting on.

"Roz, you asked me to go with you to the Bats Mitzvah and we did."

"I thought we'd do something else." Her bottom lip curls.

"No sense doing everything in the same day."

She flexes her brow. "Why do you go out with me?"

"You're my gourmada." I'm not sure what she thinks this means but it pleases her.

APRIL 6

Sunday we're playing at Van Axle Park, a playground dedicated to a local kid who kicked up a Claymore. I win the first game. Gibbons wins the second. I call Angela from a pay phone before the third game. She's pissed. I played handball Friday, took Roz out on Saturday, crawled into Angela's bed Saturday night, went to work Sunday morning and now I'm playing handball Sunday afternoon.

"I'm not a rest stop for your penis." She puts the phone down.

I lose the third game. During play, Gibbons's hands and face swell up like he's had a reaction to shellfish.

"What the hell is wrong with you?"

"I must have caught pussy-whipped from you." It's his way of objecting to my calling Angela. He accuses me of trying to break his momentum. Good idea, wish I had thought of it.

APRIL 6

Our scorebook is kept under the bar at McReilley's. One page covers a month of games. Scores have to be initialed. Clare, the bar maid, marks the book with a lipstick kiss. She's one of a staff that suggests a graduation class at Aer Lingus; girls so ripe they can be talked into pregnancy.

The mental side of handball starts long before the first serve. The times, places and dates on which we play always favor one player over another. Gibbons begins each contest with stretching exercises that hold off the opening serve. He knows it pisses me off. While awaiting him to finish his faux yoga, I'm heating up and cooling off. Serve already, Stretch Armstrong.

I don't wear shorts, he does. I don't have the legs for shorts. I tell him he's a sissy for wearing them. It's a psychological ploy to gain an advantage. I really don't have anything against them. My Dad wore shorts and he fought in the big war.

Playground basketball hurts. Elbows bump heads, fingers get jammed, and eyes are poked. It's infighting outdoors. Handball is all about grace and space. You do set picks and blocks but you're not fighting over a loose ball.

Handball has smaller players. Being seven feet tall won't automatically make you a starter. The best players I've seen have been low to the ground. High school dropouts haunt handball courts because you only need that one friend who will cut class. The two of you can play the day away. Older guys hang at the playground like gunslingers at saloons. They will play you for money. Bowling makes no demands on a grown man. Golf is for grandpa. Elton John plays tennis. Fat guys play softball.

Handball is a lunch pail sport, working class as canned ravioli and the stoop your mother sits on. Old school as sparkplugs, it remains unchanged after two world wars and an adventure in Southeast Asia. I remember watching a Hasidic dad trying to teach his little boy how to play. The father had never played the game and he chased the ball around with his hat and coat on. His son must have asked him to teach him. If they live along the Van Wycke Expressway, they're going to see kids playing handball. Rare that you see a Rabbi hit a killer.

Angela's place is on East 36th Street. The window beside her bed frames the headdress of the Chrysler building. Eleven stories below traffic flows into the Midtown Tunnel like beer into a beer glass. Angela pads around in sweat socks, panties and bra. She's smoking and arranging dried flowers. She sits on the bed and takes her glasses off. I brush her blue black hair, Archie to her Veronica. I pour on the sweet talk she inspires. I see her brow furrow over an explanation for her runaway husband.

Angela and I sleep as brother and sister. We haven't known each other long enough to assume anything. If she's not going to make a move, I won't either. Her "penis rest stop" remark is well-deserved. I lie alongside her and bite down on my mouthpiece.

APRIL 13

Spring rain chases us under the Tri-borough. The bridge provides an overhead for three courts. Rain pours down from scuppers up top so the courts are ringed with falling water. The out of bounds area is a

17

puddle but the court is dry as a cracker afloat in a bowl of bisque. The cars clanging on the metal plates overhead and the waterfalls of runoff make it hard to hear. I have to walk up to Gibbons to contest a call.

I have a hole in the toe of one sneaker and it's sucking up water with a straw. Every time I step off court, I soak my socks and pant legs. His serves go up high and come down just inside the long line. I back up to let them bounce. He's betting he can turn around in the few seconds it takes for the ball to drop to see what I intend to do. I answer with a dragon coaster arc of my own. The ball lands on the wall like a homer dropping into the first row of bleachers. He races to kill it. If he leaves a pinch of air under the ball, I cut it with a passing shot.

I win two of three games and the sulking begins. He hasn't put his shirt on.

"Play another." It takes him ten minutes to spit this out.

"Why should we? We always play three games."

"You said we should get some extra games in."

"I did?"

"Insurance games."

"I said that?"

"You're winning, might as well press your luck."

"Luck?"

My feet are soaked. I could go home a winner right now. If I lose an extra game, no progress has been made. In order to avoid Gibbons sulking I say, "Let's go."

I win 21-10; making shots I can't believe work. Mid-game he panics and makes a string of mistakes.

"Thanks for suggesting an extra game," I say

"All of a sudden you give a shit about what I want." He's putting his shirt on.

Gibbons grew up a Methodist geek who did bible readings with a church youth club. One year his complexion cleared up and he left his house a Doctor Kildare determined to cure virginity. He's entertained me with stories of getting girls in his mother's house, playing three cords of "Greensleeves" on his acoustic guitar then nailing them on the shag carpet. He played that sensitive bad boy role that requires stopping to preen in every reflection.

He had Lori on the couch while his mother came down the block carrying two shopping bags in a spring heat wave. He pulled his pants on backwards before opening the door. His mother went into the kitchen and lit a scented candle.

While serving in the merchant marine, he crashed at his Mom's bungalow while home on leave. His mother had a man living with her. He used to call me and whisper into the phone in a spy tone "Get me outta here."

We would bar hop the topless places around the airport or play chess in my attic living room. My wife set a place for him at the table. He'd stay over if it got too late. I watched him pull his tender sea stories on every waitress/barmaid who ever served us.

"Who falls for your bullshit? I ask.

We make our own line calls. I'm honest as the day is long when I'm leading. At other times I suspect the score may influence my vision. I always let Gibbons have his way in any disagreement. No sense provoking his black belt in mood. He threw a rubber ashtray at his first wife. You didn't hear that from me.

APRIL 15

Mary is Connie's best friend, Italian as Marisa Tomei. I have her on the phone.

"What do you want, puke?"

"Can we talk about Connie?"

"She's over you, after the shit you pulled on her."

"Mary, come on."

"You're a little turd."

"Seriously, you think I designed all this drama?"

"And that Valentine's Day date. How do you think I felt telling her you kissed me?"

"Mary, it was Valentine's Day."

"You make my skin crawl. You're a pussy chaser; why wouldn't I want Connie to know that?"

"Because I kissed you?"

"No because you expected me to keep it a secret from my best friend. Where do you get off thinking I care about you at all? I wish you were dead."

"Nice."

"Hang up and play with yourself, button dick."

The restaurant I took Mary to on Valentine's Day no longer exists. The Century Café on West 43rd Street, opposite the Woodstock Hotel where a crane crashed through the roof and snuffed out an old lady sitting on her bed smoking a cigarette.

Mary is a small package that can level a mailroom. Her jewelry box boasts a handful of dog tags. Her exes have support groups. She consents to let me take her out because she's Connie's best friend and her current man is married. A girl like her isn't staying home on Valentine's Day.

When she returns from the restroom, I tell her, "The waiter asked me if I wanted a drink while my daughter was in the loo." I put my arm across the top of her chair.

"Funny," she says, "Get your arm off my chair."

We talk about Connie, Connie's husband, my divorce, Mary's divorce, the fury of affairs and how single people can date married people.

"Do you draw any conclusions from what we've talked about?" I'm leaning toward her.

"Not the one you have in mind."

"Which is?"

"Get in my pants; see what the fuss is all about. Make me a notch on your crying towel."

"You're not even wearing pants." I help her on with her coat. She's wearing a tight pencil skirt knee length.

"You're not exactly complicated," she adds.

In the car she turns to me. "If you've bought me something, give it to me now."

"Why?"

"I'm inviting you in for coffee when we get home. It's how my mother raised me. If I open it there, you'll expect me to kiss you."

"That's a problem?"

It's a cigarette case, dark green marble inlay with a spring lock. Inside it holds a chorus line of Newports and a lighter thin as an eyebrow pencil.

"You can't afford this?"

"Don't remind me." I start the car.

In her house she asks, "How do you take your coffee?"

"I'll just pee and go."

"Lift the seat."

She hits her answering machine. The first three beeps are hang ups. Then men with no names are leaving breezy valentines.

"Call me on my work phone."

"Thinking of you."

"Call me at the office tomorrow, please."

"Those are the married guys?" I ask.

"Duh." She hasn't asked for my coat.

"How about a quick hug before I leave?"

"Can you do that?"

"Let's try."

My arms pin her arms. My mouth drops to hers. A kiss so quick she hasn't time to resist. Sidestepping a slap, I'm out the door without peeing.

APRIL 18

We're back under the bridge in another spring rain. Despite swilling bottled water, my mouth is dry as an ashtray. My shots are short of the wall and my serves are out of bounds. When I do hit a good shot, it seems to find him waiting for it. Twice I've screwed up the score. Gibbons sweeps me three games, each time by eight points or more. Clearly, I'm not concentrating.

I walk the earth a Frankenstein cracking sidewalk, tearing doors off hinges. My breath bubbles car paint. What gruesome behavior can be tied to me? I'm involved with two women at the same time, one married, and one single. Availability asserts itself. Maybe the one I'm free to be with is not the one I'm most in love with but fewer people get hurt this way. Angela is an antidote to Connie. Angela knew this before I ever got around to admitting it. She wants to know why her husband left without saying goodbye. If I buy dinner while she mulls it over- no drama unfolds. Our lovemaking is tame as an instructional video but I'm always ready to review it. I want to get laid as much as the next guy. Come after me with torches and pitchforks, I'm eating what's on my plate.

At McReilley's for thirst therapy, I ask Gibbons if he ever hears people from his past talking to him inside his head.

"Yeah, my Mother tells me not to play with you."

"Did you ever see your Mother nude?"

"No and I don't want to buy a picture."

"Your Mom was beautiful, a regular Joan Crawford. Did you know she did porn?"

"My Mother did porn?"

"Every one of those Hollywood starlets had to go down. Guys get a hold of a camera, what's the first thing they shoot?"

"You, hopefully."

Angela and I are at the cafeteria in IKEA.

"I've never had a relationship with a woman that didn't include a strong sexual element."

"Now you do." She's picking at her Mac and cheese.

"So you don't mind when we don't make love?"

"You're very busy."

"When I'm not busy we aren't making love. We're at a restaurant, a party or IKEA."

"So you're whining about not getting laid?"

"I'm hoping you would find me less resistible."

"You sound like a married man."

"What do you mean?"

"They always use lack of sex as an excuse for cheating."

To lead you must first serve. Jesus laid down the basic principles that infuse the sacrament of handball. In order to return you must serve. Love your opponent; he will bring out the best in you. If fouled turn your cheek.

Fundamental handball strategy is to move your opponent off the spot he wants to be on. Driving him off the court is ideal. You have to make him run for his points. Your shots should come without thought. Be, as they say – in the moment. I grunt when I hit my shots because it annoys Gibbons. He hits these rainbows that end as melting killers, It's all lollipops and soap bubbles with this guy. There's no reason to grunt if you're playing that way.

April 26

On the seventh week of the season we play in a vest pocket park between Maspeth Avenue and the service road to the Long Island Expressway. A concrete wall runs like wainscoting around two sides of a steel cage. I win the first game 22-20. Gibbons wins the second. I win the third. Local teens play us in doubles. They're reduced to smoking on court to show their indifference to getting crushed

"They're smoking Surrenders," I say.

"Did they grub off you?" Gibbons asks

I notice that I tend to win the first game, less so the second and third. If fatigue is the issue, it's a mental fatigue. Gibbon runs around in shorts and pastel tops. He once played in a housedress, don't ask me why. God knows where this kid would be if I hadn't taken him under my wing.

Gibbons is in theatre. He rubs elbows with single men in Manhattan neighborhoods where you can walk hand in hand with your handball partner. I'm from Queens; you'll look a while longer before you find an actor's workshop. If you see two guys playing handball in Long Island City, I'm the one in the long pants.

Baseball is cruel. A catcher is expected to block the plate while a runner plows through him. Outfielders who don't call each other off will exchange concussions. A second baseman will get rolled up on by a base-stealer. Pitchers brush back batters. Batters clip catchers with their backswings. These things don't happen in handball where the worst you'll ever lose is 21-0.

Touch football is frustrating. You run around all afternoon and get thrown to once. You're stuck defending a guy who never gets thrown to either. At the end of the day, you've touched the ball maybe twice. There are too many things to argue about. It's a sport for lawyers and guys who enjoy saying "Broke the plane."

In handball you touch the ball on every exchange. No one wins or loses for you. Disputes flare up but quickly cool. I give way most of the time because I'm deeper than the score.

When not dating Angela, I'm immersed in the rituals of a single guy. I don't unmake one side of my bed. The refrigerator is beer and Slim Fast. I walk the library aisles touching books I've read. I have a basement apartment with no cable TV. When I'm with Angela, we're at her place. I've shared everything with her except my misgivings. I know I'm not over Connie and I push the issue forward like an unfiled tax return. Angela senses it. Am I talking in my sleep?

May 4

The Chase Manhattan Five Borough Bike Race comes down Sixth Avenue, trapping cross town traffic in its tracks. You can't break into a flash flood of 55,000 bikes. Motorists are converted into spectators. Pedestrians have to go down into the subway to cross the street. I'm stuck in my work van. I shut the motor off and lie across the buckets seats. I'll think about Connie since I was doing it already.

"I think I want to kiss you." We were dancing to Sarah Vaughn.

"I think I want you to kiss me," she answers.

After the bikes trickle down to a stream of stragglers, traffic comes back to life. I pick up Gibbons and we play at the Ravenswood playground on a court pressed up against a Sanitation garage. The place has the funk of a laundry hamper. The back half of the court was paved with no-bid cement. The ball bounces in absurd directions. I win two of three games. Gibbons is left to bitch about the playing surface.

May 9

We are back under the bridge and away from the weather. It's Friday morning and I'm supposed to be making sales calls. Tomorrow I'm taking Roz to her niece's first Holy Communion. Sunday is Mother's Day so we play today on my company's time. If you're getting paid to do something you're not doing, it's bound to affect the way you play handball. You picture your boss driving by and thinking "Isn't that my sales guy over there playing ball in long pants?"

I once sold for a company where the guy I replaced had jumped off the Queensboro Bridge. A rule in sales: if you have had a bad day, take the tunnel. The jumper was beset by drinking and financial problems. That's the pen and pencil set of sales. Commissions move around like an Ouija tripod. You never know if your good days are making up for your bad days or if your bad years are canceling your good years.

I lose 2 of 3. I'm slow and sloppy, haunted by playing hooky. When I fall behind, I fall faster. Gibbons is in first place by one game. We go to the bar, a more traditional place for a salesman on a Friday afternoon.

Losing in handball addresses a central disquiet that pervades me. If I had a real job, a decent car, and a commitment to the Lord that went beyond doing the readings at Mass, I'd project a more confident version of myself. As things stand, when I lose to Gibbons who I know I can beat, it feels like penance. I shy from victory like a biker from a silk shirt. I could win but I'm convinced I don't deserve to.

Gibbons is a former tuxedo mannequin with a face that comes with the picture frame. He's wonder boy Jack Armstrong if Jack Armstrong smoked and wore a knee brace. He's two years older than me. I should be able to fall out of bed and kick his ass.

Roz's niece's communion party takes place in a section of Riverdale where the houses stand shoulder to shoulder on the crest of a hill. You descend a long staircase into the backyard which is a paved as a basketball half-court. We're visiting her husband's family who she hasn't seen since his funeral. She wants to walk in with me on her arm.

"You'll like them, they're Catholic," she assures me.

We park on a block that looks like Appalachia. The hatbox sized house is too small to hold all the guests. We're invited into the backyard where cold spring gusts twirl the party favors. I find a cooler of beer and stand next to it. Roz introduces me to her bereaved in-laws. The wind peels back the tinfoil covering the pasta trays and extinguishes the sternos. We shiver and greet fellow guests.

Roz goes inside, I nurse my beer. I'm picturing years in purgatory being whited-out by my agreeing to be here. One of Roz's in-laws looks like a Nam vet. He's cupping his cigarette as if wary of a sniper. With long hair and a beard, he does that thousand yard stare. He's doesn't say hello to me. He's another basket case, home without a scratch. I hand him a beer and he doesn't thank me.

The Communion girl appears in her white dress. I do that stupid Billy Crystal "You look mahvelous." I kiss her hand and call her Queen. She blushes and runs back into the house.

Roz comes down the stairs with the lace of her sneaker unloosed. I go down on one knee to tie it for her.

"Atta way Roz," from a woman watching us.

On the way home I ask, "Do you tell your family I'm you're boyfriend?"

"You are my boyfriend."

"But you're not my girlfriend."

"I know Angela is," she sticks out her tongue. "I can steal you for a few hours."

I take Angela to the hospital for Special Surgery. Run of the mill surgery is done somewhere else. The building rides the hip of Beth Israel Medical Center. Angela is having her shoulder repaired at this high-tech body shop. Last winter she got knocked down by a snowplow. There's a lawyer and a lawsuit. It's none of my business; it didn't happen on my watch.

Angela sits up doll cute in a high white bed. I run my fingers through her hair while we wait to be called to the cutting room.

"They made me take my panties off."

"Can't say I blame them."

"They said they may catch fire."

"I better double check," I move to slip my hand under the sheets.

"Can you be serious?"

"I want to climb up there with you."

"No, you don't, you're trying to amuse me."

"Amuse you? I'm here to amuse you?" I mock fold the pillow over her face.

"Hey, my shoulder."

I hold ice chips to her lips in post-op. One arm is in a sling; the other on intravenous. Angela's aunt is head nurse at Ear Nose & Throat and she's stopping by to oversee Angela's recovery. All the Filipino nurses pay careful attention to Angela. Her great black hair is fanned against her pillow. Her eyes are dulled. I kiss her cheeks and forehead, the nurses giggle.

MAY 17

We play on the courts you see outside your passenger window as your car enters the westbound tube of the Midtown Tunnel. I can't do anything right. Gibbons is killing me with his sissy shots. He's using his body as a visual block. My shots are one step short of the wall. Calling timeout after every other point doesn't help. My methods are unsound.

I'm weary from supporting Angela's recovery. It's been a week of fetching take out food and cigarettes. I'm not such a heel that I expect her to have sex with me while she's recovering. She's sure that I'm capable of being that selfish and more. I'm unsettled by a week of not sleeping in my own bed. Lack of sex is wearing ankle weights for a handball player. I lose all three games.

We skip the bar because I've promised to take Angela and her cousin Tina to the Ninth Avenue Food Fair. They are impatient to go when I arrive but I must shower first. I leave my car in the lot next to Angela's building and we cab to the fair where I eat things I don't have a prayer of digesting.

At a window table in a dark bar, a United Nations of girls passes outside.

"Can you keep your eyes indoors?" Angela asks.

I pull the two of them into a huddle over the table.

"I don't want the whole place to hear this but I've taken a careful look around and you two girls are the fairest of the fair."

"Good." Tina smiles

"He can ice chip your lips too." Angela pinches my arm.

Tina is staying with Angela so I'm free to go home. When I get downstairs I find my car is locked into the lot. I stare through the cyclone fence at my hostage Riviera. Like a kid who screws up running away from home, I return to Angela's and sleep beside her without touching.

While turning your hips into a shot, you pivot on your big toe so that's the point on your sneaker that wears out the fastest. I've played with my big toe peering out like a mouse from a mouse hole more than once. You've got to buy a new pair of sneakers at least once a season. Other than that, this sport is inexpensive.

I bring Gatorade to the court and Gibbons brings water. We don't offer to share our drinks should one of us run out. Resupply is an ingredient in war.

Gibbon's cream puff style brings me toward the wall. In handball you don't want to be close to the wall, you could bump your head against it. Chiffon shots of his kiss the wall and die. I feel like I'm wearing a potato sack as I lunge after them. They evaporate under my hand and I swear to God I see him smirking. Losing my temper I call a long time out. I walk around the edge of the court muttering. Then I pull my shirt off, suck my gut in and run back on the court. This cracks Gibbons up - my plan all along. Now I'm hitting my shots with newfound authority. I'm not going to let him push me around with his cotton candy style. Do I need to remind this man I'm the 1996 Interboro Handball champion?

May 24

Last night I went to a party at Angela's aunt's apartment. We acted as a couple and her family seemed to approve. When we got home, we didn't make love. I know how to get along without sex, I was married once. Celibacy is not going to contribute to my comeback in handball. While seducing Angela's is its own reward, I can't ignore a suspicion that it will make me play better.

I lose two of three games. Gibbons is begging me to play an extra game; he wants to amass a twenty game lead. It's absurd but he talks like it isn't. No one has ever compiled a twenty game lead.

"If I broke a leg, you might have a 50/50 chance."

"Do you remember the last time you won?"

"Awhile ago - so what?"

"It's getting late early."

"Copy, Yogi."

When I'm with Angela, I think about Connie; where she might be and what she might be doing. I know at times she must be making love with her husband. Angela's not making love with anyone except me but there are long intermissions between acts.

Driving around during the day, I picture myself pulling up next to Connie at a light. I touch my eye, my heart, and point at her. Peeling away like fighter pilots, we race to a Jones Beach parking lot. Once she's in my car, there is no thought of going outside.

May 26 is Memorial Day. Angela and I watch my Mom accept her Gold Star Mother bouquet at the Floral Park town square. The town assembly honors my older brother lost in the war. My family likes Angela;

she's quiet and beautiful to look at. I take her to the movies to see LOST WORLD, a dinosaur epic. When she smokes, I light her cigarettes. Watching her bend toward the flame makes my mouth dry. The first time I took her home she reset the stations on my car radio.

Mary calls.

"How is Connie?" I want to know.

"What do you care?"

"Mary, please."

"You ruined her. Don't act like you don't know that."

"I love her."

"You screwed everything up by not showing that day."

"There was nothing I could do about it."

"Bullshit, you bastard."

"You called me. Please tell her we need to speak."

"That's not happening. I have to pick her off the floor every time we talk about you."

"Do you think I want this?"

"Why didn't you show up?"

"I swear I couldn't."

"Why?"

"On that day, it wasn't possible."

"You told her you would always be there for her."

"I still say that."

"You're a lying sack of shit; you just string words together."

"Please ask her to call me."

"Fat chance, you're history."

"I don't believe it."

"Write it down Moron; she hates you."

"There's got to be something I can do."

"Yeah, drop dead." She hangs up.

My limited experience suggests that no woman passes up the chance to slam a phone down. It mimics throwing a drink in your face across an area code.

Two minutes later the phone rings.

"Mary, is there a name you forgot to call me?"

"Shut up. Here's what I want. Tell me why you didn't show up that day."

"What difference does it make?"

"If you want to speak to her, you have to tell me."

"If I tell you, don't tell her. I'll explain it to her myself."

"Promise."

"I was with Angela at the time."

35

"I knew it!"

"We were in Bayville that weekend."

"Oh shit."

"See what I mean?"

"You couldn't make an excuse and come home?"

"I didn't want to lie to her."

"Hello, do you hear yourself?"

"It was our first overnight away date. I didn't want to start lying about things."

"So lie to Connie."

"I didn't exactly lie."

"You didn't exactly tell the truth."

"There was nothing else I could do."

"You suck, you chose someone else over her."

"Angela has nothing to do with this."

"You're with her now?"

"We're dating, I don't live with her."

"I hope you sleep soundly.

"I don't sleep at all. Can't you get Connie to take my call? Come on Mary, please."

"You're a walking bullshit machine. I take my promise back. I'm telling Connie where you were."

"Mary, please don't, let me tell her."

"You'll never get the chance."

Three months without speaking to Connie gives me stomach cramps. Lori and Mary are her lawyers. They see what I hope Connie doesn't; that I'm high risk/low reward. I'm unworthy because I didn't show up on March 9 when everything happened on the same day. .

Back on February 10, Connie called to tell me she told her husband that we were having an affair. She decided that we were not going to see each other while they went to marriage counseling. I took Mary out on Valentine's Day to talk about what Connie had done. Angela was mad at me for not taking her out but I explained that this date was made before we started seeing each other.

To make it up to her, I take Angela to Bayville on March 8. We get a room in a beachfront motel deep into the off-season. We walk the windy beach. I push Angela on a swing and take her picture with the Porky Pig statue in front of the novelty shop. We eat at Steve's pier, lobsters and margaritas.

In our room she puts on plaid pajamas and we lie on the bed in the light of a muted TV. I kiss her as you would the head of a newborn. We're a world away from her apartment and the city outside her window.

I get up and double lock the door, strip, and get back in bed. I start to sing but she stops me with a kiss. Her hair falls over my face. I'm Magellan on R&R in the Pines - post circumnavigation.

In the morning I leave her sleeping and go to get coffee. My beeper goes off, it's Connie. I call her from a pay phone on the wall of the deli. Her voice is unreal after weeks of not speaking.

"I want to see you."

"Today?" I say it too loud.

"Tonight at Mary's, we're going to talk."

"I can't."

"What?"

"I have church and all."

"Church? I can't believe this. Okay, after church."

"Fine but..."

"But what?"

"Nothing, you just caught me by surprise."

"Are you with your girlfriend?"

"I'm at work." I scratch a line on the deli wall, one line per lie.

"So what's the problem?"

"No problem, thanks for calling."

"Are you coming?"

"Of course. How are you?"

"Ask me tonight."

With coffee, I return to the room. Angela is sitting up in bed watching Meet the Press.

"What took so long?"

"I had to find a place to put air in my tire." I scratch a wall inside my head.

Twelve hours later Angela looks puzzled as I pull up in front of her building without parking. She hugs me and thanks me for the weekend. I took her to brunch in Oyster Bay after Connie's call. I did my best to not seem preoccupied and I think I got away with it. We hit a couple of garage sales, stopped so I could take her picture at the Roslyn duck pond and visited my Mother. After Mass we went to the wake of my co-worker's father.

While in church waiting in the sacristy, I call Connie from a phone in the Pastor's office. I lie about a car problem on a priest's phone. She slams the phone down after I hear a rattle in her throat. When I walk out on the altar to do the readings, I see Angela sitting in the second row. I never told her about Connie's call. I didn't tell Connie I was with Angela. I had promised Roz I'd meet her at a restaurant later tonight. After I whisper my contrition, I take communion, on my knees I ask the Lord, "What the hell am I doing?"

I take the Tri-borough Bridge back to Queens and Peter Luger's restaurant on Northern Boulevard. The valet has a wine stain on his white jacket. The night has wound down to a handful of tables. Roz is sitting beside Bill across from Henry and his girlfriend. I plop down as a fifth wheel.

"Traffic is so bad squeegee guys are doing oil changes." Bill laughs, the others smile. Bill is visiting from Miami.

"Roz has been telling us about all the nice places you've been taking her."

"Regular jet-setters, we are." I pour myself some wine,

We all worked for the same export company a dozen years ago. We start trading Roz stories which requires another round. They tease her about her man-hungry years before getting married. She turns pink at becoming the topic of the conversation. She slaps Bill on the arm like a high school girl

The party is ahead of me by a dinner and desert. The wait staff circles to remind us we're the last table in the place. I get Roz in my car after a string of goodnights like a movie scene with a half a dozen takes.

"I was sure you were standing me up."

"Wrong," I say.

"Not by much."

"Bill would have taken you back to his motel."

"He didn't offer."

"And if he did?"

"He's married."

"In Florida."

Roz is babbling from the drinks. "I can't believe you showed up."

"I said I would."

"But you missed dinner."

"I'm going vegetarian."

I stop in front of Roz's house, not shutting the car off.

"Aren't you coming inside?"

"Roz, you wouldn't believe the day I've had."

"Tell me inside."

"I'm dead. I have to go."

"You spent the weekend with Angela. What do I get an hour?"

"Please Roz."

She sits not touching the door."

"Really Roz, some other time."

"Bullshit."

"I'll never be able to sleep with your barking mutts."

"I'll put them in the yard."

"They'll bark in the yard."

"Okay, take me home with you."

"Roz, please don't break my balls."

"If we don't do it tonight we never will."

"Promise?"

"That hurt, ass wipe."

"Sorry Roz, it's a joke."

"Eat shit and die."

On the Southern State Parkway, I do a body count. Angela is mad I didn't stay over, I stood Connie up and Roz is pissed at me for being a smart ass. When my CHECK ENGINE light begins glowing like a Jack-olantern, it tips the canoe on a day where everything has happened. March 9 is March 10 when I get home.

MAY 31

Angela joins us at the St. Vartan's court at 36th Street and Second Avenue, across from the parking lot that kidnapped my car. She smacks the ball around with a borrowed paddle. Gibbons and I watch her ass, honed by step aerobics. Guys on the basketball sideline follow her somersaulting ponytail. She hits a shot off the court and smiles like a TV anchor. After a kiss, she's off on her own schedule.

"I sleep alongside her," I think to myself. The first time I met Angela I couldn't speak for two days. I was married with kids and sick to my stomach waiting for the fever to pass. Fast forward fifteen years and I have my own socks and underwear drawer in her bedroom. The wild card is that Roz invited me to a party where Angela and I got reacquainted. We were both recently abandoned.

Gibbons calls our meeting to order. The winner of last week's contest serves first. I'm aware of the moves he uses to jump out to a quick lead. It's like watching a boy scout do card tricks. I pretend to be fooled. All I have to do to prevail over this dude is to avoid self-imposed limitations and guilt enough to fill a water glass.

Imagining where Connie is and what she's doing, I lose the first game 21-12. I'm so far behind in the second game that by the time I shake the blues I've lost two. In the third game I finally prevail. The Gibster gets on his bike and pedals home.

"How did you do?" Angela is watching a black and white movie when I get back to her place.

"Can I take you to dinner?"

"You lost."

"Cause I was thinking about you."

June 8

Lori tells me Connie is in Paris. I picture her in a chair by a window watching rain run down an outside wall. Her husband and daughter are asleep on the bed. I dare to think she's thinking of me. I'm in McReilley's after losing three games.

"Don't bring your girl to the game," Gibbons advises.

"Was I talking aloud?"

"No, but you want to. You're using her as an excuse for losing. You don't want to say I'm the better player."

"I'm in sales; I've told bigger lies than that."

I'm a salesman don't discount what I have to say. If my company enjoyed any advantage over its competitors, there would be no need for me. I make up the difference between what we are and what we say we are. You're willingness to do business with me validates the whole purpose of my being. You are special to me. The guy in the deli who makes my coffee, the shoeshine guy, the kid who pumps my gas, I don't see them. I'm their customer, you're mine. I drop everything to take your call. I'm your new best friend with complimentary golf-tees.

June 15

We are at Treewood Playground in Astoria. Two handball walls stand apart like bookends on an empty shelf. The great red castle of the Steinway Piano factory looms over the neighborhood.

"How was your son's graduation?" Gibbons wants to know.

"By the time I got there, it was over."

"You didn't take off from work?"

"I couldn't and then I got caught in the worst traffic."

Gibbons frowns. He doesn't own a car; what does he know about traffic?

"You missed your son's high school graduation?"

"Didn't we just go over this?" He doesn't have kids.

"Did you see him afterwards?"

"Yes, I did. He said, "Don't worry about it Dad.""

"You don't treat him any better than you do your girlfriends."

I recognize this as his cheap psyche out meant to piss me off just prior to his opening serve.

"Fred McMurray - get a kid then we talk, in the meantime, serve."

I lose two games. Without fervent prayer, I might have lost all three.

June 21

Gibbons, the Gibber, Gibbonie he uses these handles among others, when referring to himself in the third person.

He bikes from Manhattan to Shelter Island; its a hundred miles and a ferry ride. It takes him seven hours to get there because he stops to smoke. When he arrives he waves off the theatre group he's supposed to meet with. He describes his thighs as throbbing jungle drums when he calls to cancel handball.

"You are a mental case." I'm doing Ralph Cramden.

"It would have put you in a hospital."

"No doubt. I wouldn't drive that far."

"Gotta push the envelope, Amigo."

"No you gotta play handball."

"We'll make up the games some other time."

"So you forfeit?"

"I could afford to. I'm up nine games."

"I don't need your stinking forfeit."

"So it's not a problem?"

"Wrong, bike-shorts breath; it's a big problem."

"Pedal out here if you insist on playing."

"Stand on one foot while you wait for me."

I'm in a tar pit of car problems and sales fatigue. I hold the open mirror door of my medicine cabinet nose to nose with my nose.

"Wake up you fat loser, crybaby, wanker, wimp. Quit with the excuses – do something right for a change. Get your car fixed and hit a few good shots. Ditch the weepy mood, period boy. Can you make one fucking sale? Can you do that much?"

Salespeople often have to give themselves a talking to. That's why we're called self-starters. Don't look for encouragement from your boss; he's wondering what he ever saw in you.

I meet a guy who runs a wood tank company. He has five thousand pounds of knocked down park benches and planters he has sold to a condo development in Fort Collins, Colorado. I get the transportation bid for $7,000. It costs my company $3,100 to move the material. Now I'm taller, walking around the office with my back straight. I'm too cool to high-five. My car needs shocks and brakes but I'm in a position to have the boss eat some of it. I would love to talk to Connie without having to lie to Angela about it. I resolve to restore sanity in handball this weekend.

On my office day, I call Lori.

"When are you coming to New York?"

46

"Wednesday night, my brother-in-law is picking me up."

"That used to be my job."

"You used to be a nice guy."

"Thanks for remembering. Are you staying with your sister?"

"That night I am. In the morning I'm going to my parents place."

"Let me take you and your folks to breakfast."

"Why?"

"I want to see you."

"Is it okay with Angela?"

"I'll slap your skinny butt."

"Blah blah blah."

"Angela says that all the time."

"She knows you're full of crap, I'm sure."

"You'll like her."

"I don't want to meet her."

"Lori, please."

"I'm serious. Don't even think of bringing her."

"What about Connie?"

"What about her?"

"Can you get her to take my call? I need to speak to her."

"Aren't you putting a lot on your plate?"

"Oh my God, that's how salespeople talk."

I take Lori and her parents to breakfast at the Tower Diner. We sit in a booth overlooking Union Turnpike. The menus we flip through are thick as wedding albums.

"Aren't you supposed to be working?" Lori's Dad asks. He's a woman's shoe salesman, smile, charm, silver hair.

"Taking your daughter out is work."

Her Mother is a bird-like. Seated next to Lori, her feet don't touch the floor. "He loves to tease you." She touches Lori's hand.

"She has a PHD in teasing," I say.

"Mom," Lori sighs."He wants me to help him get in touch with a girl he dumped. Otherwise he wouldn't be here with us."

"You are such a cruel little witch."

Her folks smile at each other. They seem sure some of this is serious. The waitress arrives. Lori's folks are regulars here. They ask about another waitress.

"She's our favorite," Lori's mother announces.

"She starts at 11, do you want to wait?" The waitress puts the menus on her hip. It's 9.30 am.

Later that day Connie calls me. We have a date to meet at Mary's house. Thanks Lori.

June 29

48

Erected on the graves of rails that once took coal cars from the East River to the Hunts Point Yards, this park paves over the history of Queens. To the New York City Parks Department it is the Greenpoint playground, we call it the Lost Ball courts.

Three cadet grey courts stand shoulder to shoulder against a factory wall. Their outlines are drawn with blue primer. Any shot over the wall is lost on the factory roof.

I'm bouncing around throwing punches. Connie's call has me on fire. We're going to meet at Mary's tonight. The Gibbster is studying me. I must have a look on my face. I haven't told him about Connie.

I start hitting shoulder high shots straight to the wall, no spin, no angle, no thought of killing. Just the piston firing Larry Holmes jab that your opponent can't always avoid. Gibbons is hitting a lot of shots off court. He puts two balls on the roof during the first game.

I win the first game 21-11, the second 21-17'. I'm muscling him around; I'm so focused I'm scaring myself.

"Did you read a book or something?" he wants to know.

"Say what?"

"Tony Robbins, did you sleep with Tony Robbins?"

"Shouldn't you call time out if we're going to chat?"

I lose the third game 21-19. We go to the bar.

"Someone put a feather in your ass?" Gibbs hands me a beer.

"I'm seeing Connie tonight."

"God bless."

The blue of a handball is darker than sky blue and lighter than blueberry. It's a royal blue. You find handballs in a plastic bag hung on a nail behind the counter in a bodega. Buck a ball is standard. They are made in Taiwan and come to Queens by sea. Green, yellow, rarely red, but the majority of the time a handball is blue. Don't ask me, I don't make the rules. Spaldeens are not for handball. They're for stickball. Stickball went out with your neighborhood Travel Agent.

At the hour of a summer evening when light is so muted you can't tell the expression on a face ten feet away, I try anyway. They are standing on the stoop like catalogue models. They may not be smiling but I'm smiling. I hurry up the walk and put my arms around Connie. Mary turns away.

"You two come inside. I'm going to bed."

Connie and I sit in the breezeway. The night crowds around two candles on a glass table. There's a neon blue bug zapper in the corner. Connie is whispering with tears in her eyes.

"I hate you," she says.

"I hate me too."

I stand her against the wall, my knee between her knees. I know every furrow like Uncle Sal knows his garden. I guide her mouth to mine. Her kiss is like sniffing glue.

I squeeze her breasts and feel her nipples beneath her summer gown. I kiss her nose.

"Are you wet?"

"Oh God, shut up."

After doing everything we can do standing up or sitting in a cane chair, we straighten ourselves and say goodnight. Mary waits in the house, a disapproving big sister. I run to my car. No details as yet but Connie and I are back together. After five months, I've dislodged the sourball stuck in my throat. Now I'll kill in handball.

I call Connie at work the next day. "Please tell me last night was for real."

"You've called at a bad time."

"Meet me after work, the spot."

"I can't stay long."

We go to Inwood Park, a finger dipped in Jamaica Bay. The planes come down so low you can see their wheels unfolding. We're sitting on a blanket behind a line of fir trees.

"You went away with that woman."

"Do we have to? It's such a nice day."

"Twenty eight days with us not speaking and you're off on a honeymoon."

"Mary told you that."

"Of course she did."

"It's not like it sounds."

"I wanted to see you that day."

"Don't you think I wanted to be there? I told Mary, everything happened at once."

"You said you didn't want to lie to her."

"Yes, I said that."

"So you lie to me." As if to engage in arm wrestling, her hand comes around and before I react she takes off one side of my face. I lie down on the blanket, ears ringing; she hit me a shot that would have been gold in handball.

July 2

Today is Wednesday in my vacation week. We are playing at a Maspeth park. It's the "spiral staircase" because the courts are pushed against a curl of cement walkway that leads to a pedestrian overpass for the Long Island Expressway.

It's July hot. I win the first game but may have overextended myself. There is a rope-a-dope element in handball. You don't want to show all your cards in the first game. I often tweak my serve and change the side of the court that I'm serving from. Gibbons has a couple of little ploys, nothing I haven't seen before. He takes his shirt off to spook me with his third nipple.

I lose the second game but come back to win the third. Between the last two games, I take a break at a play area where I'm not supposed to be unless accompanied by a child. I'm soaking my head under a mushroom shaped sprinkler intended to water toddlers. Shelter moms in shower caps guard their strollers. From ringside benches, their voices carry across the park. They glare at me when I wave at their kids.

Timeouts – there is no rule that dictates the number and length of timeouts a player may call. Macho sensibility doesn't allow for any one player taking a breather after every volley. If you're on the ropes, take a knee, wipe your face, mock-tie your sneaker. Anything that changes momentum is a worthwhile tactic. Should a ball from an adjoining court pass in front of you, play stops. This is not considered a timeout. If you call a timeout, you must call a time in when you are ready to resume. In the event your opponent is serving for the winning point, it's understandable that you might "ice" him by calling a last second time out. Doing this twice in a row tests the boundaries of good sportsmanship. No thought should go toward using it for a third time. In a well-played game, there shouldn't be more than two or three timeouts called; anything more indicates a degree of gamesmanship that flatters neither player.

July 6

Back at St. Vartan's Park, across from Angela's, we are witness to a city empty for the holiday. The heat index is 105. Gibbons and I are smacking the ball around on a court adjacent to where the homeless pretend a latrine. The breeze carries the reek of excretion.

We are alone in our activity. The bums on the benches have snaked themselves under the arm brackets so they appear to be casualties strapped on gurneys. Not one of them stirs against the heat - like jungle cats they can't be bothered during the day.

I lose two of three and without ever having the lead. We go to Sandy's Bar at Second Avenue, dark and cool as a movie theatre. The Yankee game is on the flat screen.

I call Angela and invite her to join us. I drink one beer and then run out to meet her. I find her standing outside.

"Three months ago you would never have let me walk over here alone."

"You're here already," as if I'm uncertain that she is.

I run to buy her cigarettes. She goes inside to drink with Gibbons, something else I would never have let her do. I appear unable to disguise a growing indifference.

The big Gibbonie is writing a screenplay on spec about a bar called Coyote Ugly. I bring Angela and her cousin to meet Gibby and his wife at the scene of the screenwriting. We are sitting in a booth that might have been wiped down in a past life. The girls want margaritas but the bar maid makes a face. It's not that kind of bar. Everyone gets Corona.

Gibbons's wife is an actress with dreamy eyes and a skunk white stripe through her black hair. We clink bottlenecks. Gibby is sitting with his nose in the air as if sniffing a plot.

The barmaid exhorts her regulars. "Did you people come here to party? Stay home and beat the bishop if you can't make some noise."

The crowd does an early evening whoop. Men call out their pet names for drinks as she pours shots. The jukebox plays drinking songs and guys with cowboy boots stomp on the wood floor.

"So?" I'm looking at Gibbons.

"Nothing yet."

"He's soaking in atmosphere," his wife explains.

"Is that what I'm sitting in?" Gibbs says and the girls laugh. He doesn't amuse me. I've suffered his humor for years.

The crowd does a countdown to the barmaid knocking back three shots. I turn to the girls.

"Makes you glad you studied in high school."

"Don't you wish you did?" Gibbys's zinger is aimed at me.

"Don't make me bring up the Queens College Writing contest.

"You've already brought it up a million times."

"One million and one."

Gibbons is my competitor. If I diminish him, I devalue my victories. It's no big deal to beat a guy who sucks. It is only in beating the best that we excel. He's not the best but he's the best I have. I don't have time to recruit others. Gibbons is my competition supplier and he comes with the expense of putting up with his stupid stretching, half fag apparel and sulking like Hamlet.

Ray is Gibbons's long lost brother. He deals cards in a Reno casino. Whenever he's in town, we trade kid brother stories. He tells me how Gibbo once held him in a headlock for three hours.

"Imagine the smell of his armpit."

I tell Roy how my older brothers would fart on me. "God forbid Mom made potato salad."

Roy and the Gibb once played on the same Pop Warner football team but Roy wouldn't block for his brother. He explained it to me this way, "Let pretty boy get his own yards. He broke the hearts of girls whose ass I'd kiss if they ever said 'Hello" to me. By the way, don't introduce him to your wife."

"Now you tell me?"

July 14

We celebrate mid-season at an east side court squeezed between a U.N. parking garage and the F.D.R. Drive. The north side of the wall is shaded by a Dutch elm. It's 95F. The only other people in the park are a family of immigrants huddled around a drinking fountain. A working water fountain is so rare it draws a following. By default they are our audience.

We begin running around in heart attack heat. I've gulped down all my Gatorade by the end of the second game. When Gibbons goes off court to retrieve the ball, I put his water bottle in the sun. In war neutralize enemy resources. Poison the wells. I lose the first two games.

His serves comes off the top of the wall so I have to look up into the sun to compose my return. He uses my shadow to read my approach. He slashes shots to the side where I'm not. If I hang back, he hits baby taps to the base of the wall. If I charge, he tries to hit the ball past me. A few times in the game he stops to ask if I'm alright in a way designed to unnerve me. I'm breathing heavy; it's not against the rules.

I call timeout and go to the fountain. The Russian family is speaking Russian as I approach. They watch as I slurp water and wet my head. It occurs to me, they think this fountain might run out of water. They have filled up several water bottles.

"Let me ask a question." We're at the bar after I lost that third game.

"Oh crap." He makes his face.

"This is not about me; it's about a friend of mine."

"I'm your only friend," not the first time I've heard this.

"An old friend, someone you've never met."

"Sure."

"He wants to know if getting used to a girl is the same as falling out of love with her."

"Is Joyce Brothers on vacation?"

"Seriously, your thoughts."

"Tell your friend that the woman he moves toward when he's drunk is the one he needs to be with."

"Why?"

"Sober, you're going to be affected by consideration, maturity, and a sense of acting responsibly with the lives of others."

"Drunk?"

"You're going to listen to your inner child."

"Wow, professor."

"I graduated Queens College, remember."

"What were you drinking?"

"Same thing my inner child was drinking."

Gibbons's advice is like porno. After the first few minutes it's what you thought it would be –useful in a limited way. I'm dancing on a glue trap in areas other than handball. I need to decide on a direction. Between Angela and Connie, I can't enjoy either of them as much as I would if the other wasn't around. I'm a team with two quarterbacks.

Dave Greenfield is a U.S. Foreign Service officer stationed in Thailand visiting New York on holiday. He's friends with Tina and Angela and is escorting them to the Philippine Trade Show. I offer to get lost but Angela insists I accompany her.

Dave is a young man too polite to admit his feelings for Angela. I can see from across the room that he's in love with her. I like him right away. He hands me his card and I hand him mine. If he was wearing a tie, he'd be ready to work. We take a cab to the trade show. It consists of cheap booths manned by travel companies and cell phone suppliers. Visitors are invited to sign up for credit cards and ten minutes of massage. Stalls sell Filipino food and soda in cans. I plant myself in a corner where I can watch women climb the stairs. I see Dave and Angela walking the aisles; he's tall, she's not. A Filipino woman in a business suit approaches and hands me her card – Ladies of the Orient. I hand her mine.

"You enjoy Asian women?" she wants to know.

"I hope its not showing."

Dave and Angela pass as we're talking. Dave has his hand on the middle of her back. Tina is not with them.

I haven't won a set of games in the past month. It's 100 F and the borough of Queens has gone to the beach. Gibby and I are the final two contestants in a dance marathon staged on a hot plate. The sun sparkles as a disco ball. I have my hands on my knees while holding down puke. Heat waves rise around me, sweat streams into my ears. I pour water down my pants. Gibbons is moving in slow motion. He's run around more than me; that's why he's winning.

At McReilley's, the record book shows I've lost two out of three. The air conditioner chills my damp underwear. The Gibster is in the can powdering his nose. Our beers stand on the bar, golden and cold. I wonder if I should start without him. The barmaid has returned to her Sunday paper. In the dark quiet, I can feel my heart beating. The afternoon is a fat lazy housecat, quiet as the All Star break. I leave my beer alone. I'll wait till he returns and toast his victory. Losing is no excuse for bad manners.

"Here's something I'm proud to announce. I've never sat through Swan Lake."

Gibbons shakes his head; every statement I make, he feels obligated to challenge.

"Your resume says you have a B.A."

"Don't start with the college stuff."

Gibbons graduated Queens, I didn't. I took Lori as my major and pursued her from cafeteria to Rathskeller. She was pretty as a geisha, her full lips and wide smile drew admirers from every corner of the campus. I loved the feel of her fake rabbit fur jacket from Great Eastern Mills. She became my thesis. The girl befuddled guys twice as smart as me.

"I'm listening to you put down classics while you pretend to be educated about them," Gibby for the prosecution.

"Beg your pardon, Deano. You got a degree so you could go to sea and chip paint."

"Want to touch my sheepskin?"

"Day's not over, dude. I could go back and finish. Remember I won..."

"Yeah, the book about the toaster, hooray for the Hemingway of pop-tarts."

"You get your ass kicked in handball so you start waving your diploma around."

"I'm ahead by 11 games."

"Oh that

"I don't want to waste your time," my sales target offers.

"I don't want to waste yours."

"So why would I schedule you."

"They pay me to call on the movers and shakers in traffic management. If I skipped you, I wouldn't be doing my job."

"Nothing will come of it."

"It won't be the first time."

"I don't have time to waste."

"Let's set a date now and not waste anymore."

"It will have to be after the first."

"Okay the second; morning or afternoon?"

"Afternoon but I won't have much time."

"I understand, two or two thirty?"

"Three but call first, just in case."

"I'll be there. If something comes up, chances are I won't be able to reach you."

"Fine but no promises."

"The second at three, I promise."

"Okay, I've got another call."

"Before you go."

"What?"

"Thanks for talking to me."

An appointment is to a sale as a date is to a love affair.

Connie and I can't be alone for five minutes without frisking each other. Our meetings revolve around secluded parking areas. It's all heated unbuttoning since we've being seeing each other again. Of course I don't say anything about this to Angela. I'm hoping she doesn't notice my conflicted mood.

I take Tina and Angela to the Chelsea Market. Tina buys a lobster big enough to be a house pet. I buy wine and flowers. Tina has sold her condo and is moving in with Angela. She'll sleep on a futon an arm length away from Angela's bed.

"No making out while Tina's with us," Angela proclaims. It's not like we were knocking out the bedsprings before this came up.

Back at her apartment, Angela has no pot big enough to hold the lobster so the girls leave on a scavenger hunt. I lie on Angela's bed thinking of Connie, moonlight on her thighs in the back seat of my car. The girls return with a pot borrowed from a pizzeria. We eat on the coffee table, cracking the lobster with a toy hammer. Angela and Tina are laughing and smiling, their lipstick is melted butter.

Connie and I have eaten in this diner so often the waitress is like an aunt to us.

"She says you hate women." Connie is quoting her therapist about me.

"You believe that stupid bitch!" I drop my fork for effect.

"Why can't you be serious?"

"We were apart and we didn't like it. Now we're not."

"You're with Angela too."

"You're with your husband."

"I'm married."

"I'm not."

"It's too soon. He's not ready. I'm not ready."

"When you are, it will be only the two of us."

"I wish you meant that."

"I wish you believed me."

"You only wanted me in bed."

"In the beginning."

"You'll sleep with Angela this weekend."

"Stop."

"I can't."

"I'm not married to her. We don't live together."

"Do you tell her you love her?"

"No."

"Why?"

"I don't want to lie to her."

"But you lie to me."

"I love you."

August 3

Gibbons stages a theater project where plays written by high school students are performed by professional actors. It's not as bad as it sounds. He spends the middle of the summer dealing with artistic temperaments. When he shows up for handball, he enters as a white mouse in a boa's cage. I sweep him three games. The scores are in our scorebook, available for inspection upon written request.

Roz shows up at my apartment.

"Can I go to church with you?" Mass is 6.45 Sunday night.

"No Roz."

"Why not?"

"Because you're Jewish."

"Jews can't go to a Catholic church?"

"Of course not."

"Why?"

"You guys killed Christ, remember?"

"No, we didn't."

"Then who did?"

"The guy from the Bible - Poncho Pilot."

"Is that the Spanish Bible?"

I take her with me to church. From the altar podium, I watch her squirm in the third row. She's a step behind everyone else. When it's time to shake hands with the people around you and say, "Peace be with you," she thinks it's the collection. She's handing money to strangers.

Doing sales out in the sun sucks. If I don't make my calls in the morning, the afternoon is a steeper climb. If I don't get them done in fair weather, I have to work in the rain. Traffic is bad, my shoes are wet, and my hair goes Kramer. My enthusiasm is a wasting Tinkerbelle. Clients are suspicious of salesmen not smart enough to stay indoors when it rains.

I'm lucky enough to get face time with a client who is annoyed to see me. My flawless opening unfolds with the right amount of pause, punch lines on their marks. I say the client's name and the name of his hometown. I cite examples where people doing business with me experience unspecified rewards. I dismount to imagined applause. He shakes his head as if to say that he might have been moved on another day but not today, not in this rain.

August 10

We're at Spirit Park, a playground attached to St. Roman's school. I win the first game 21-11. Gibbons is sluggish. He's hitting his shots off court. Once I have a lead, I play it safe. I win the second game 21-10.

"I'm going to sweep you," I say.

"Good luck."

Midway through the third game Gibbons hits the ball into the street. I take a breather, sitting on my heels like a guerilla in a third world rice paddy. There is a strip of grass that separates the court fence from the sidewalk. It's an area ignored by the Parks Department. The grass is a foot high and lush from a diet of dog turd. The breeze presses it down as if it were being flattened by a landing copter. Looking up, I see the Gibb waiting.

"You alright?" He bounces the ball to me.

I make a big deal about placing my foot on the serve line. There is the issue of a foot foul which I have never called but he's down two games and could be that desperate. Technically you're supposed to serve from behind the serve line. I serve at the nexus of the sideline and serve line but have seen Gibbons move toward the center of the court to gain an advantage. You're not allowed to serve behind you. These rules have evolved over a lifetime of playing. I'm not sure if they've been written down.

"Stay awake or you're sweep goes south." Talking to me just before my serve is one of his tactics. I lose the third game 21-15.

August 16

In a bitter contest on a Hell's Kitchen court, I lose two of three games. Gibbons snaps at me for serving before he's ready. It's a trick he's tried before. He follows that up by taking the ball with him when he steps off court for a timeout. I'm left standing at the serve line like a jilted groom. These tactics are designed to cool me off. Another move is to call "Time out" just as I'm starting to serve. I win the third game anyway.

At Angela's I shower and dress. We go to Secret Harbor, a restaurant in the lobby of the Shelburne Hotel. The lighted steeple of the Chrysler building shines down on our window table.

"He tried every trick he could dream up." I'm telling her about our games.

"Who did?"

"Gibbons," is she listening?

"You thought I'd be interested?"

"No, of course not. Let's talk of something else."

Angela has settled her lawsuit with the snowplow for twenty thousand dollars.

"My cousin wants me to go to Turkey with her," she advises.

"Great, what am I supposed to do?"

"Play handball."

"I thought we weren't talking about that."

"I'll be gone for two weeks. Can you take care of my place?"

"Are you asking me if I know how to water plants?"

"You'll do fine."

"Without my best friend?"

"Gibbons is your best friend."

"If you could play handball, I wouldn't know him."

"If Connie was single you wouldn't know me."

I take back any pretense that I've disguised my feelings. After every adventure, I catch drama. I've got to push on with this project of two girlfriends - like a guy who decides to house paint in August.

In sales your handshake is your serve. Get over with it and your victory is in range. You can only score while on offense. Putting your target on his heels can open the door to your controlling the call. We've all been well met - the rest is details.

I've hardly varied my handball serve all season. Always an underhand shot into the far corner of the court. I hit hard and try to keep the ball up in his eyes. Gibbons jumps around serving from both sides of the court in the same game and changing levels. I have the stubbornness of a fire- baller. Now that I'm behind eight games, I see I might need to improvise. I start using a dead ball serve and a kind of matador move where the serve passes very close to my body. The mechanics of these moves must remain confidential.

Gibbo and I disagree on most issues but shake hands on the idea that I expect to beat him and he expects to beat me. It's why we play the games.

August 23

Gibster is vicious after losing two games.

"Did Angela help you color your hair?"

I make a big deal about looking in the rear view mirror while driving to the bar.

"I've got the same five grey hairs I had when I graduated college."

"Graduated?"

68

"You don't lose well.

"When I see streaks of Grecian Formula on your tee-shirt, it throws me off."

"You got your butt kicked; why pretend it hasn't happened before?"

"It's hard to concentrate when you're seven games up."

"Ali Baba, the alibi guy."

Sales is the application of personality in a business exchange. Faced off against a better product or a lower price, the salesman is expected to overcome his competitor's advantage. The weaker the position of a company, the more it needs a clever salesman. Don't hire away your competitor's top salesman because he's used to being in the lead. You need a guy who can come from behind. .

Mr. Powers understood sales. He handed me a check for $1,000 with no explanation. I'm not going home early anymore, calling in sick, getting jury duty or finding another excuse not to work. The check is an amphetamine suppository. I shake his hand.

"You're the man."

"I'm a fool or a genius; you're going to show me which."

I'm ready to walk through walls for this man. There is no break-even in sales. Ties are losses. Sales is show business and your most important audience is your boss. Find out what makes him laugh, raises his mood or makes him look good in front of others.

"I didn't lose any business," is my entrance line at the end of the day. Mr. Powers is fond of saying, "I'm paying you to breathe."

If you can't bring back work, bring back snacks. Little donut balls or cheese sticks for the staff. Your return to the office is a formality. The staff is sure you've been screwing off all day –they're not stupid people.

August 27

I lose two of three games at the outdoor sauna of the Tunnel Courts. Gibbons is urging me to continue into a fourth game. When you're playing well, you don't want to stop. I'm obliged to go to my corner and take a breather.

"Let's stick to the schedule, Cowboy."

"Of course, Angela's waiting."

"You're married; you can get home anytime you want."

He's makes the stupid whipping pantomime.

"Of course, but we're finished for the day."

If you can do anything else, don't do sales. Be certain you'll never master a tool or figure a way to be paid to shuffle paper. If you were meant to do anything else, sales will drive you back into the arms of it. Once your head is in the sales bucket, breathe deep. If you're still doing sales after one year, you're successful. If you're doing sales after two years, you're a failure. Sales is work you work away from.

Connie is disappointed if I turn my head toward other women. I know she watches them, why can't I?

"Looking is not chasing."

"It's disrespectful."

"No, it's not."

Connie pats my hand.

"Concentrate on handball, loser boy."

"Who told you to say that?"

I'm at Angela's apartment. She's leaving for Canada to visit her cousin; I'm taking her to LaGuardia. We make love before we leave because I'm sure I'll want to make love to her as soon as she's gone. Her nervousness about air travel animates her lovemaking. I do a Captain's voice-over while on top of her

"Attention passengers, engage your life vests."

"I'd enjoy it, if you were serious sometimes." She's smoking a cigarette in the car.

"Of course." I squeeze her hand.

Angela's dad was a salesman for Beechcraft. His plane disappeared over the Philippine Sea. She wore a party dress every day that he was missing. When the wreckage was found she hung the dress up. She now prefers jeans and boots

"Thinking about your dad?" I ask her at the gate.

"I'm wondering if he knows I'm going out with a salesman."

"He knows."

"Does he know if you're true to me?"

"Whoa; salesmen don't share that kind of thing with other salesmen."

"I'm not in sales, share it with me."

I pull her close and put my face in her hair. I lift her arm and start kissing her wrist like Gomez from Addams Family. I'm acting like I've answered her question.

"My Belle, My Beauty." I'm using a stupid accent.

"You're crushing my purse," she says, pushing me away.

"Don't I wish?"

Sales has parallels with weightlifting. Days you skip negate the days you don't. If you tirelessly pursue the skill, it will change the way you walk. You'll find you're able to move people more easily. You don't have to exert yourself; the way you shake hands, the way your suit fits, people sense your power. Your smile is a muscle flexing. You're good at this stuff when you don't have to think about it. Repeating prescribed motions creates results.

In handball as in chess, you have to move your opponent. He's going to stand where he wants if you let him. What you make him do determines what you do. Set an intelligent trap. If you are thinking about what you're doing, you're doing something wrong.

It's Labor Day. Angela is with her cousin in Canada, Gibbons and his wife are in L.A. and Connie and her husband are in Vegas. I'm driving under a sky that is Tiffany gift bag blue. Clouds assemble at the far west horizon. I could have walked to get my coffee and paper. I have all the time in the world today. I'm going home to lie on my couch and reflect on my worst handball season ever.

September 13

I'm slapping arcs at the wall. Giant rainbows that brush the face of the wall, light as a showbiz kiss. Gibster has California sand in his Adidas. Panels of light, shaped as playing cards, slip down from the elevated tracks and across the windshields of passing cars. We are playing at the Astoria east courts where the N train oversees the contest. Across the street from the Neptune Diner, we're close to the ramp for the Tri-borough. An upstate a breeze swirls through the Hellgate and up to Hoyt Avenue where we stand shirtless. I smell apples.

Today I own my opponent. I muss his hair and knock his books on the floor. When I'm playing like this, I never argue a call. I know this is my day and all I have to do is relax and await victory. All I ask of Gibbo is to play his best and let me keep score. I'm quick to credit his determination because after all it flatters me. I win all three games. His five game lead is fragile as a Faberge egg.

Being involved with two women at the same time is a sand trap that has ruined better golfers than I'll ever be. Angela suspects I see Connie, Connie knows I see Angela, why aren't I enjoying life more? Angela is affectionate but not passionate, Connie is passionate but married. Everything with her is intrigue and secret codes. We once kissed so hard I thought I cracked a crown. Angela is milk and cookies and the TV at the foot of the bed. My faith is weak as a Hard Rock cocktail. I may have to pray my way out of a situation I prayed myself into.

Connie is going to California to take a mud bath with Lori.

"Would your girlfriend let you go?" Connie asks.

"Am I invited?"

"You'll tell her you're going with me?"

"I'll tell her I'm going."

"See what I mean."

September 27

Gibbons objects to what he considers gloating. I'm skipping around in a circle waving my tee shirt. I've won two of three games at Treewood Playground. I feel like I could bench press a Steinway.

"You don't like losing do you, Joe College."

"Not like you, dropout breath.

"I have credits in my sock drawer."

"You blame Lori for failing at college and Connie for failing at handball, do you see a pattern?"

"Yeah, you just lost two out of three."

"I'm four games ahead of you, dumbass."

Arrogance is the Gibster's favorite accusation. Imagine me arrogant. I'm humbler than the humblest person he knows. Shorty Pants wouldn't know humility if it bit him on the ass. Get a load of him calling me arrogant. Some kind of graduate school reverse psychology shit he's trying to pull. Won't work, Wonder boy, I've forgotten more about humility than you'll ever know.

October 4

We're playing on the west side of Astoria Park. I won last year's championship game on the east courts of this park. My final shot in that game ended in a seamless slap of palms.

It feels like August with a useless breeze. I blow my nose on the bottom of my tee shirt. It's raining but not hard enough for us to stop playing or move to a sheltered court. Gibbs wins the first game. In the second game I watch sweat beads drop off my nose like paint beads from a brush. I'm hitting great shots. I win 21-18. I lead in the third game until he calls a timeout I never heard him call. It negates a great serve and changes the momentum. He comes back to win 22-20.

I stop at Roz's house. I haven't heard from her in weeks. It's time for her to stop being mad. On the way up her walk, I can hear her dogs yapping. I'm never sure if she has three or four. They are penned in the kitchen where they screech and leap up like heads in a bop a hippo game. They will bark without rest while I'm around. Roz opens the door wearing a robe that must have strained the world's supply of terrycloth.

"Hey stranger." She's wearing lipstick.

I kiss her cheek and sit in her Lay–z-boy. Her living room looks like someone is either just moving in or about to move out. Groceries are stacked on the coffee table. Roz opens her robe to show me a valentine red teddy and stockings stretched to just above her knees.

"I have a date coming over."

"Who's the lucky guy?"

"His name is Vito. You don't know him."

"He bought you that outfit?"

"He's a fence man. He repaired my fence and we got to talking."

"Anything else?"

"None of your business, you're with Angela."

"I don't think it's a good idea to have men come over your house when you hardly know them."

"I know him a little."

"You're desperately horny, aren't you?"

"Why else would you stop by?"

"Roz, I've never laid a finger on you."

"You don't think I've noticed?"

She pulls her robe closed.

"I have a man coming over."

"So you want me to leave?"

"Another time would be better."

"Okay, how about never?"

"Don't be a sorehead. Tell Angela "Hi".

October 12

"Happy birthday, Gramps." Gibbons hands me a glass. It's a tradition that he acts like I'm older than him. I just swept him three games at the Lost Ball courts. Two games weren't even close.

"Technically my birthday is tomorrow," I add.

"At your age, you can't assume tomorrow."

"You're sore about losing."

"Think of it as my birthday gift."

"You're not that generous."

"I'm up three games. You would have to sweep me again just to get even and that's not going to happen."

"You're sure?"

"Does ten yards make a first down?"

October 18

Gibby and I are in the truck I use on my weekend job. We're in a line of drivers waiting to unload at the Hilton Hotel on 54th Street. Union goons walk around with walkie talkies. The hotel is hosting a campaign fund raiser. Gibbons is slumped in the passenger seat reading a book. I'm jumping in and out of the truck to make sure no one is cutting the line. I know Gibbons thinks this is my sneaky plan to throw him off his game. We'll be at least an hour late for our opening serve. More if the line doesn't start moving.

"The easiest thing in the world is to love a woman; the hardest is to love two."

"What?" He looks up from his book.

"I felt like saying something profound."

"Keep trying."

"Do you understand why I'm not playing better?"

"No credit goes to me?"

"I'm tied up inside, guilty about being so fortunate."

"Have you been drinking?"

"No, I'm just talking because I have nothing to read."

"Try the writing on the wall."

Gibbons wins two of three. I play reckless trying shots that don't have a chance of working. I sense a curtain closing.

Angela and her cousin get on a plane and go to Turkey. I'm ashamed of being so indifferent about it. I buy a farewell round at the airport bar and try to seem forlorn. They kiss me and are gone for two weeks. I look forward to being alone and playing handball.

October 25

The grand finale is at the Cow Palace.

"You can forfeit if you're scared," I advise Gibby as he sits on the court, pulling on his toes like a Yogi doing yoga.

"You have to deny mathematics to win."

"I sweep you three, then what?"

"You're still one back."

"You have to win by two games."

"Bullshit, who ever said that?"

"It's in the book."

Earlier in our season, he was up by as much as thirteen games. I've crept back into the contest. I'm a four win streak away from a whole new me. Angela is away for two weeks. Connie is with her family. Roz blew me off for her new guy. I'm alone in the world with my mission. Tonight is the Ladies of the Orient party I've been invited via email. I'll flirt with women I've never met. How nice I'll smell if doused in victory cologne. I win the first game.

"Sometimes talking about what's on your mind can help." He hates this kind of ball busting but I have to do it. It contributes to keeping him unbalanced.

I lose the second game and then I lose the third game. I get a consolation hug from Victoria, the barmaid. Our handball season is over. It's time to set the clocks back.

We've played 99 games and 47 times I came out ahead. I'm looking at Place money. I'm happy for Gibb. If he had blown a thirteen game lead, he would have cannon-balled into a pit of self-pity. Chances are he would have written another play that I'd feel obligated to sit through, maybe something as tragic as his waffle iron.

"I owe you a trophy, mate."

"My shelf is starting to sag from awards."

"Gracious of you not to gloat."

I stumbled through the first third of the season when Connie and I weren't talking. After we got back together, I bounced from Angela to Connie and back. It's not a recipe for good handball.

If I like you, I'm predisposed to like the décor of your house even before I've seen it. I was nuts about Angela when I first met her. Walking beside her, I was high-fiving streetlights. Her smile just melted me. She never flat out said she didn't like making love but how could I explain her ex leaving? Something bit him on the ass; I can't imagine he met anyone better looking than Angela

Her apartment décor leaves me unmoved when I move in. She doesn't believe in hanging things on the wall. Of course I have stayed over before but suddenly being alone in her place feels creepy. I looked at her underwear drawer and say, "No" aloud. The thought crosses my mind that I am alone in an apartment in Manhattan for the first time in my life.

Hemingway said, "A man can be defeated without being destroyed." I didn't graduate college, excuse me! But what I think Ernie is getting at is you don't have to push anyone's face in the mat like Gibbons does to me. He once held his brother in a three hour headlock, sorry if I told you that already.

The Ladies of the Orient party takes place in a basement event room at a restaurant within walking distance of Angela's. There's a thirty dollar admission. I don't recall that being mentioned, like Gibbon's phantom timeout, I go along with it. Downstairs, beautiful Filipino women are walking around in high heels and party dresses. After your first drink, it's a cash bar and you're supposed to buy the girls drinks. I'm not stupid but the thirty caught me off guard. I don't have enough money on me.

The other men sit alone at their tables like I'm sitting at mine. We look like delegates from a Losers Union. The stirrers come over and ask which women we would like to meet and talk with. I ask her to ask someone else first as I need time to choose. I love the black hair and white teeth of the girls. Not all of them are young but even older Filipino woman look young. I'm nursing my free drink. The other guys look like limo drivers, bachelor uncles, and older dudes shopping for geishas. Do I belong here?

I rise and excuse myself as if I have people at my table. I run upstairs to the ATM. This is going to require more than one drink. I promise myself to stay an hour and no more. Of course I'll dance and buy drinks. Let's party, I'm a single guy.

The main floor of the restaurant is filled with people out to dinner. I start back to the party when I see her sitting alone. I had watched her downstairs earlier dancing with a guy old enough to be my dad. She is taking a break and drinking a cup of tea. It takes two steps for me to stop and change direction. Something in her smile is setting off my smoke alarm. I'm sitting at her table talking like a salesman, touching my fingertips to the table like I'm playing a Steinway.

Her name is Estralla, it's the Spanish word for star.

Lingas to Carlisle

In appreciation

Rotary International

Who conceives the Lord's intent?

The Book of Wisdom

My story begins with a door closing. Bill escorts me into his office. He closes the door behind us. I take the chair beside Tom on the visitor side of Bill's desk. Bill sits opposite us leaning forward on his elbows. He's only making eye contact with me. I've muted the sound because I'm being fired and nothing being said will change anything. It's the Tuesday before Thanksgiving, a traditional doldrums in transportation sales.

I've been canned before. I was fired from one job twice. Another time I got the axe three days before Christmas. I had just got home from buying a tree. My head has rolled in the back seat of a car after a sales lunch. Most times I've been fired its taken place in the same office I was hired in. That's the drill today. Tom is here to observe .Bill is gesturing with his hands and I'm nodding my head. It's important to help the man firing you get through it quick. It's more stressful to fire than be fired.

As a salesman, I'm trained to turn events to my favor. Playing good sport about being quick kicked allows me to exit head high. It increases my chances of getting my last paycheck on time. Salesmen don't sweat this kind of thing. Sweat is the cologne of a working man.

Each time I've been fired, I've felt an immediate sense of exhilaration. The conversation results in my opportunity to work for any other company in the world. To a veteran salesman, every flooded pothole is an in-ground pool. We see the glass as full.

Standing to shake hands with Tom and Bill, mine is the only dry hand. A sales force is set free. I leave the room a free agent

In the northeast quadrant of India (Bihar), the holy river Ganges rushes south fed by the sweat of Everest. In springtime the raging waters dislodge giant Himalayan stones and carry them south along the river floor. The stones get knocked smooth as they travel hundreds of miles before coming to rest in the lowland shallows of India. There they turn against sand and smaller stones for a Maha Yoga (great age). Picture a bowling ball spinning in a bowling ball polishing machine for a thousand years. When the stones are smooth and tear-shaped they are "lingas". They can weigh up to 70kg and at that size will sell for $20,000. The stones are worshipped in Hindu temples by the disciples of the divine Shiva.

Shiva is the Hindu God of Destruction. The linga is his phallic icon. Linga means phallus, as if a phallus mimics a tear drop. Religious scholars have asked aloud why a God of Destruction would be linked to a symbol of procreation. The rest of us have no trouble tracing the destructive path of the penis. Who hasn't witnessed a family torn apart or a life redirected by the appetites of the little king? History is his story. Dictators have generated mischief throughout the ages. The God of Destruction welcomes an association with the author of so much discord.

The most sacred lingas are fished out of the Ganges. From there, they are exported across the globe. Let the record show, I brought lingas to the Hindu temple in Carlisle, Massachusetts.

Sales is an away game. You're not an office worker. You get in your sales car and drive to a sales call where you try to sell someone something while sitting in their stadium. On the way, you rehearse, recall what's worked in the past and limber up inside yourself. Breath-spray, check your hair in the car window and your teeth in the rear view mirror. Shine your shoe tops across your calves, with a business card locked and loaded, stride inside. Act like you're there to pick up a check long overdue you. Ask for the man you're here to see.

"He's not in today."

"We have an appointment."

"Something must have come up."

"Wouldn't he have called me to cancel?"

"If it was important I'm sure he would have." She hits you with her gatekeeper smile.

Outside, you enter traffic exiting the parking lot. There's a stop and go drive ahead of you and you have nothing to show for it. Two thoughts crowd the front seat of a salesman – Am I making any money? Am I going to be fired?

Salesmen live a life that hides from the world they inhabit - apologies to Thoreau. A salesman sells the company he wishes he worked for and offers the level of service he wishes his company could provide. So not to pollute his vision of his company with the behavior of his company, he stays out of the office.

Bill has fired me at the instruction of Tom who considers me disrespectful. We disagree over the treatment of my client Surrinder. Tom insists we inflate our fees to screw the guy and I won't go along with it. A salesman must be loyal to his customers. Without them there's no reason for him to be on the payroll. His paycheck could be the boss's car payment. I go against Tom on Surrinder's behalf because it's the right thing to do. Surrinder is my client; Tom is the owner's son.

The firing is predictable. I have a sixth sense about getting let go. That's why I've taken steps to insure Surrinder is protected. We have several transactions underway. I can't let my client's interests be held hostage in a billing dispute. My appetite for the hand that feeds me obliges me to advise – keep your resume warm if your path in any way parallels mine. Surrinder is a Sikh entrepreneur. He started an auto parts business in his hometown, Bokaro Steel City, India. He made his living selling brake pads in a state intent on making steel. Along with everyone else in India, Surrinder looked forward to coming to the United States. When he and his wife moved to Bayside, New York, they found more than enough auto parts outlets and no steel mill. He became a stone dealer. I asked him why.

"To make money." Sikhs have no tradition in dealing stones. They are a caste of equipment operators but don't say that to their face.

Sikhs are the kickass sect of the Hindu religion. Guru Govind Singh founded the Sikhs in the seventeenth century. He formed them as Guardian Angels, young men who patrol the streets in funny headdress. They are a warrior class, a posse that steps in when their religion is getting pushed around. Muslims and Mongols bully Hindus. Frail from fasting and meditation the Hindus are slow prey. Their tea stalls get kicked down and their bus passes stolen. Sikhs swear an oath to protect Hindu festivals and temples regardless of who's officially in charge of public safety.

In order to look fierce Sikhs never cut their hair (kach) which gives rise to their turbans and rolled beards. A silver bracelet worn on their right wrist (Kara) protects them from harm. They carry a small silver dagger (kirpan) in case long hair doesn't scare you. A special undergarment (kish) and a wooden comb (kangha) complete the 5k's. Not a Do Wop group - the 5k's are a way for a Sikh to checklist himself before leaving home.

In India Sikhs dominate the state of Punjab, named for a punch thrown by a comedian.

I first meet Surrinder when he opens his door. I've knocked at his apartment; a sales man trying to make a sale. My story takes shape with that door opening. His eyes lock onto the silver bracelet on my right wrist.
"Where did you get this?"

"Patna," I answer.

"Come in." It's an insult for a Sikh to do business in a doorway.

The floor of his office apartment is covered with circles of loose stones spaced as the colors on a Twister tarp. The walls are pegboard draped with vines of necklaces. A computer, a phone, a fax machine and a postage meter huddle in one corner like a drum set. On a straight back chair, I sit and watch him talk on the phone. When you arrive unannounced trying to sell something, be prepared to wait. Surrinder issues demands to his caller to demonstrate to me that he is a deal-maker with limited patience. I see his wife in a side room, sitting on the floor stringing beads. She's wearing traditional Indian dress. I resist any urge to fidget. The more time you spend in a Sikh's house, the more likely it is he will do business with you. Surrinder hasn't even asked me what I'm selling.

I'm in Queens selling export services for an Italian freight forwarder in Newark, New Jersey. The owner carries competitors in the trunk of his car. I work for his stepson Jerry who's so fat his sides are rubbed raw by the arms of his swivel chair. At an airport loading dock, I copied Surrinder's name and address off a crate awaiting export to Belgium. I go straight to his place. In sales - don't let leads go cold. I read his full name off an envelope at his door, Surrinder Singh Sonni. All Sikhs have a Singh in their name. It is the Hindu word for lion – Sikhs are the lions of India.

By the time fat Jerry fires me, Surrinder and I have turned my cold call into a warm relationship. We have put together a string of exports where my company makes a little money and Surrinder makes a little better money. It's not a good idea to advocate for your client at the expense of your employer. Jerry doesn't think it worthwhile to curry (ha ha) Surrinder's favor.

Surrinder starts adding chores into our relationship that bring no reward to my company. I'm getting paid cash by him at the same time I'm being paid by my employer. I'm cheating on my job and the IRS. I'm drawn to his welcoming Sikh bear hugs...

"Pretend you've sat here for an hour telling me what a great company you work for while you run to the bank and take care of these transactions." Surrinder hands me his attaché.

My love of India is a benefit to Surrinder and he takes advantage. We never talk about the possible consequences of me taking time away from my real job to run errands for him. From the time I've spent in India, I know a wise man makes a Sikh his friend.

Junior year of college, I take part in a student exchange to India. My collection of poems about famous prisons and prisoners won a school-wide competition. That earns me the poet slot in a crew of five art majors. Dave is a dance teacher, Frank paints, John is a musician and Randy runs a theatre group. Our group leader Gordon is an associate dean at St. Johns. In India our host is a man named Tagore, whose family is to the arts what the Rockefellers are to the Christmas tree. Our adventure is underwritten by Rotary International.

In Patna, a Sikh guru slipped the Kara on my wrist as we toured his temple. I've worn it ever since. Twenty years later, it gets me into Surrinder's world of moving stones. I don't want to jinx myself but I haven't even had a shaving cut since I put the thing on. There's a distinction between a raspberry, a bruise and a contusion but you'll have to ask someone else.

I get fired from the Newark airfreight company soon after Surrinder and I start making big numbers. Jerry is not happy that ninety percent of my revenue stems from one client. He wants me to have more than one ball in the air. I try to explain this to Surrinder but he only assigns me more responsibilities and pays me in cash. That isn't the issue that sparks my dismissal. I'm fired for my big mouth.

"Go ahead Jer, it doesn't show on you." Fat Jerry is hesitating at the dessert table. It's the company Christmas party and too many people laugh aloud. He catches me at the men's room.

"Stay out of the office – we'll mail your last check."

"Jer, it was a joke, we're at a party!"

"You gave me the boost I needed to get rid of you."

Surrinder uses my firing from a company as an excuse to not pay invoices pending on the day of my departure. It's a show of loyalty that saves him a lot of money. Surrinder never shares his windfalls but he doesn't let me starve either. After Jerry boots me, I go to work for Bill and

Tom and bring Surrinder along as my number one account. After Tom gets a whiff of the money Surrinder makes through our assistance he insists on raising our service fees. He suspects I'm doing too much for too little. When I don't go along, Bill comes to escort me to his office.

When you're without a job, you look at working people with keen interest. Many employed people seem less grounded than you - yet you're the one with nothing to do. You can afford to sit at Dunkin' Donuts and drink your coffee while it's lawsuit hot.

I pull up to the house where home used to be. My daughter is out the door in a windbreaker and jeans. Her long straight hair mimics her shape. She's fourteen and straight up and down as a steam pipe. She's carrying her books and gym bag. Her chauffeur hasn't shaved.

"Good morning to you, good morning to you." The same stupid song I sing every morning ending with, "kiss ca se la padre."

"Dad, did you get fired?"

"What makes you say that?"

"You haven't shaved; you're not wearing your suit and you have all this junk on the back seat." A clever girl I have - this young Rose.

"I may be changing jobs if I get the right offer."

"Should I tell Mom?"

"No, I'll tell her." The five minute ride to high school seems longer.

"Will I still be able to take karate?"

"Of course you will." I promised to pay for it

Surrinder's brother Rampal lives in Bokaro and runs the auto parts business while changing currency as a sideline. He learns of lingas for sale at a nearby native village. With a roll of rupees and American cigarettes he closes a deal to purchase the stones. Carrying one stone the size of a football in his lap Rampal leads a procession of bike cabs back to Bokaro. There the stones are crated and painted with Surrinder's Bayside address. Twice before Rampal has tried to ship lingas but wound up holding worthless dock receipts and bogus bills of lading. This shipment is arranged through an agent in Bombay. It involves trucking the stones across the beltline of India.

Exports require a shipper and a consignee. Just as a love affair, it takes two. You can't ship without a ship-to address. If my desire to buy what you have is greater than your desire to sell it, I pay the freight. You could roll the cost of transportation into your selling price but I may elect to pay the carrier directly. There might be a situation where my desire for your goods disappears while they are in transit. When the steamship line sends me an arrival notice and advice of charges due, I may take the position that retrieving the goods is pointless. Perhaps I've lost the buyer I intended to sell your stuff to.

In Bokaro, Rampal loads the lingas on a truck decorated as a temple. The cab is strung with tinsel. Amber and green running lights outline the truck body. Indian truck drivers are non-union. They drive for as long as they like, high on betel nut and local teas sold at roadside stands. Rampal has the nervous stomach of a shipper using a gypsy carrier. He wires Surrinder - 500kg by sea 90 days. A week after they arrive at Port Newark they remain unclaimed. I have intercepted the arrival notice and kept it secret from Tom. It is disrespectful but I had a feeling I was going to be fired.

The afternoon after I packed up my desk, I drive Surrinder's truck to the St. George warehouse in Port Newark. I arrive without an appointment. I'm wearing a business suit in a dungeon of abandoned cargo. This is a G.O. (government order) warehouse where goods that haven't cleared customs get stored. There's stuff here that nobody is ever coming after.

The coffee truck sounds its horn. I buy for everyone present. I'm paying cash for the storage fees. It's the day before Thanksgiving so no one is paying close attention to my paperwork. I'm tipping everyone who comes near me. When the forklift sets the crates on the loading dock, I see a four foot drop from the dock to the bed of the truck. A Forest Gump floor sweeper comes to my rescue. Together we affect a controlled drop of the cargo into Surrinder's pickup. I pass him six bucks for his assistance. When I reach the Holland Tunnel on my return I can't find a $50 bill I'm sure I had. I realize I tipped my helper $56. It's an omen pronounced as a nose pimple.

96

I hold my first linga when I get back to Bayside. Cracking open one crate I pull out a stone the size of a Nerf football. It's heavy as a bag of nails. Grey, green and blue strata come awake when Surrinder's wife applies 409 from a spray bottle. .

"Two hundred and fifty," Surrinder estimates its value as if I had asked.

"Really?"

"These are temple quality stones."

Surrinder's wife shrieks when one crate contains a 120lb linga. She and her husband begin an animated exchange in Hindi. They go inside the apartment and I wait for his signal to follow. When the conversation levels off Surrinder calls me in. His wife is making tea.

"I sold these stones to the temple in Carlisle for $10,000. Now I see that one stone is worth more than that by itself. If I give it to them they will resell it and make more money than me and I've done all the work."

I nod to show I'm following.

"My wife says we keep the big stone and send the others to Carlisle. I can't give away $20,000."

"Who can?"

"This is a business decision. You take the stones in my truck to Carlisle. They will pay you $400."

"That's generous," I say without conviction. "How do I explain the missing crate?"

"That is for you to think about on the way."

"So you need a salesman to cover your crimes."

I've retrieved the stones through a sleight of hand by which the company that just divorced me becomes liable for the destination fees. Six hundred dollars and change - Tom and Bill will be furious when they find out. I expect it will take a week before the issue arises.

Four crates contain middleweights that I'll take to Carlisle. The fifth crate contains one heavyweight that Surrinder values above all the others. I have to ask myself "Am I getting paid enough?"

We drag the giant stone into the garage where it sits alongside crates of quartz and crystals. The other four crates stay on the truck. I listen as Surrinder smoothes his client's feelings over the phone. The stones are four months overdue and the client has asked for his money back more than once. Surrinder assures them I will be there on Friday. They want me to come up right away No way am I driving on the day before Thanksgiving

The Clearview Expressway is a major thoroughfare that does not enjoy the volumes other highways boast about. It is rarely mentioned in traffic reports. Northbound it is an access to the Throg's Neck Bridge, southbound it funnels into a traffic light on Hillside Avenue. Driving in that direction is like passing your car through an eye-dropper. With four crates in the cargo bed I sail Surrinder's Toyota pickup, north to the Bronx. It's seven am on the day after Thanksgiving. The sun is sleeping off a turkey dinner .A fog thick as a Q-Tip hovers above me. The drive is six hours up and six hours down according to a wild guess I've made. We're driving to Carlisle, Mass. via Connecticut and Rhode Island. While waiting for the sun to punch in I'll spin tales of not getting laid in India.

Return with me to the winter of 1982, I'm sitting in the upper room of a house in Cuttack, State of Bihar, India. In the thick part of a ninety minute hour I'm felled by homesickness, I sit and stir melancholy like a mixed drink. Stacks of time sit like chips on a poker table. I imagine I can hear my blood circulating. In the double quiet of this siesta hour, I descend to a deeper silence. I taste saltwater.

"Are you crying?" Gordon asks.

I sit upright. He has broken the moment. Why didn't I hear him on the stairs?

"Just meditating," I wipe my eyes.

"Well join us; we're off to a gelatin factory."

I don my red Rotary blazer and grab my notebook. It scares my mates when they see me with it.

The gelatin factory is in the rear of a small train yard. It stinks of carrion and smoking tools. In the office there's a small altar of garland and candles supporting a guru baseball card. Out the window we can see a shed of carcasses; past that a fuel tank shaped as a giant hockey puck. I'm imagining ghosts of the dead animals throwing a party in the yard when the workers are gone. Dave frowns as he sees me scribbling ideas. We're in the back row of a small congregation. John and Randy are up front asking the director questions.

"How old are the animals that are brought here?" Randy asks and no one knows why.

"Can you get older than dead?" Frank answers and Randy shoots him a look that says, "I wasn't asking you." The rest of us laugh because we're tired and wondering when we'll eat.

India is a nation of poets. There are more people than jobs for people to do so many men are left to play the art card. I meet a holy man with the flapping step of a stroke victim. He's wearing a cloth not big enough to cover my kitchen table. Putting my hands together in greeting, I try to smile a holy smile. I want my Rotary host to ask him a question. He assures me the man understands English.

"Guru, what is poetry?" After all, this is what I'm supposed to be doing over here.

"Whatever you seek, you have found." I stow that away to be considered at a later date.

Among the arts, poetry is the easiest to dismiss. It is too indulgent with its creators. People suspect poets string together lines of gibberish and who can say it isn't legit? In that respect, the discipline shares a seat with sales. There are no rules. No one with real ambition spends their day doing sales or writing poetry. Unless you're in India - where I hear this story that illustrates how India elevates its poets.

Swami Vivekanand (1863-1904) was the Bruce Springsteen of Indian poets. I arrive in India ignorant of the man, like a Hindu comic deplaning in New York to ask "Who is Seinfeld?" People seem surprised at how uninformed I am. I try to make the distinction between studying poets and writing poetry with limited success.

In September of 1893 a parliament of religions convenes in Chicago. Mr. Swami Vivekanand represents the Hindus. To the group of conventioneers he spells out the concept of dharma – a preoccupation with living out ones prescribed role in life. He rattles the returning lunch crowd by proclaiming "Christ and Buddha are but two waves on the boundless ocean of I am."

Clergy and politicians are representing American religions; India has sent a poet to explain its beliefs. Thoreau is dead and can't comment. The American hosts are put off by the chauvinism of this towel-head and send him home with cool formality. Americans are not avenged for his hubris until Ginsburg goes to India.

On your Hagastram, I-95 rises as a surface to air missile from New York to an area west of Boston. At that point you commit to the city via I-93 or go west to the sleepy burghs of Wellesley, Concord and Carlisle. Walden Pond is a popular stop – swim in designated areas please. Two lane roads with names like Ice Pond and Deer Hollow double-stitch the countryside. Thoreau would survey up here and while he did he searched for the arrowheads of the Penobscot Indians, one time locals. I go to Carlisle on behalf of India Indians who have founded a Shiva temple – as much an outpost as a Burger King in Calcutta.

Join me jumping rope on the rooftop of the Patna icehouse. The rope passes overhead like a bird in the corner of my eye. With my legs and stomach burning, I change speeds and improvise steps to stay interested. When the rope catches my heel, I lay down with my chest heaving. Staring up into a blue afternoon, I see myself as the center of the universe. Last night Gordon quoted Thoreau, "There must be the copulating force of love behind every individual effort."

I wish he hadn't put it that way. We're in India two weeks and celibacy is chafing like a new shoe. I think I know what it's like to quit smoking.

India is a brown country. The air is brown and smells of outdoor cooking and farm animals. Dust is the national condiment. Baby tornadoes swirl down streets where the populace suggests a fire drill on

Noah's ark. I'm here to study the poetry of India for seven weeks, like being given a night to understand the stars.

I'm a shooting guard in a five man squad coached by Gordon. He is our group leader. His silver hair and quick smile mark him a natural diplomat. We're sarcastic college students and fine art majors to make matters worse.

John, our center, is close to seven feet tall. He may be the tallest man in India. He's a musician at Julliard. He doesn't like basketball and won't even play in a metaphor. People flock around him and touch him and he deals with it with charm and dry humor. One of his hosts asks a carpenter to extend a bed to accommodate John. Looking at the measurements the craftsman says "No such man." Once we hear that, John owns the title.

Gordon, our leader, has an unholy attraction to Henry David Thoreau. A high school acid trip launched him into a career of teaching and writing about Thoreau. He's excited that our group knows so little about his subject. As the poet in the mix, I'm ashamed to say I didn't know Thoreau wrote poetry. I do write poetry but hold a gun to my head if you expect me to read anyone else's.

India is the birthplace of race and religion. From the north of India (Bihar) Aryans moved east and south. They mingled with darker races in the south and paled with the tribes of the central steppes. Compelled to move further and further away from home; they carried in their overnight bags mathematics, astrology, and love of the arts. From the early pages of a history book, Middle Easterners plunder Aryan kingdoms for loot and booty. Art and culture have no answer for hordes made horny by months on horseback. The bullies of each age are seduced by the passive aggressiveness of the Hindus. Seeing every event as the will of God spoils an oppressor's mood. After Gandhi read Thoreau, he got the British to leave India with the deft touch all salesmen aspire to. I've skipped a few things but this is snapshot history. People who get paid to say things have said "India is the womb of the world". In its villages, life is as un-changing as the sex organs.

.

This drive to Carlisle recalls a trip in Bihar. Dave is squeezed between John and me. He is our Lord of Dance. Light on his feet as a featherweight, Dave carries a handkerchief sprayed with cologne to mute road odors. His college thesis is on Chhau – the masked dance of Serikella which plays its home games here in Bihar.

During our first two weeks in India we have been treated to a hot belly dance and a recital where a kid dressed as the Jack of Diamonds dances on the edge of a brass dish. There have been dances of welcome and farewell, dancing at dinner parties and dancing at festivals.

"Dance is occasioned by no specific need. It is man's three-dimensional instinct for rhythm. It is the Mother of all arts. Gestures are the vocabulary of dance." Dave is rehearsing his after dinner speech.

Dave's a single guy better looking than a lot of women. He attends Columbia University while making a living selling real estate and teaching ballroom dance. He lobs this observation.

"India is a land of a thousand dances."

"Boney maronie!" John and me a half beat behind.

While practicing lane-changing I consider my response to the issue of the missing crate. The crates are marked 2 of 5 and 3 of 5, so there's no sense saying we only shipped four. The client has copies of the paperwork and it all reads five. A linga doesn't break. They may see themselves due a partial refund and expect me to accept less money. My story better hold holy water or I could wind up broke in Carlisle on Black Friday. I've got to find the temple, spin a story, grab the cash and get home. The money is for Rose's karate.

"The face is a distraction in dance. A mask insures that the limbs alone portray emotion. If you've ever danced at a Halloween party you know how hot a mask can get. Picture the discipline required of these dancers leaping around swinging heavy swords while wearing false faces."

Dave expounds further on Chhau dance as if we were still interested. Chhau means mask in Hindi. Frank is disappointed when told that all dancers are male.

105

"It is too arduous for females and too important in a culture where women are not welcome in the arts. Men portray Goddesses in tales of epic lovemaking. In the off chance you're following me, I'll flip through the origins of Chhau."

"Before modern redistricting Seraikela was a self-contained entity in the state of Orissa. The mountains that ring the kingdom protected it from the gangs that overran the rest of India. Its army had time on its hands. To amuse their Maharja, the Serikela soldiers devised sword dances that told of what they would do if any enemy did make it over the mountains. This becomes a tradition for the army and more fun than close order drill. Fast forward a couple of generations and meet Kumar Saheb Bijoy Pratap Sing Deo, the modern day Guru of Chhau dance. He takes the art in a new direction. Doing away with the swords, he begins retelling the Hindu story of creation in masked dance. He introduces the "lasya" element to dance. In it men imitate the graceful sexual movements of women."

"The army must have tied up its privates." I can't go five minutes without trying to be funny. It doesn't deter Dave.

"Chandrabhaga is the dance that tells the tale of the Sun Temple in Konarck. We will be visiting next week. A moon maiden is skinny-dipping at dawn at the beach at Puri. Her body bedazzles the Sun God rising on the east horizon. Before he can get to second base the God Kamadeva (Cupid) shoots an arrow of sexual repulsion into the moon maidens butt. The Sun God is all over her with hands and French kissing. Rather than be raped, the maiden swims out to sea and ends her life in the surging ocean. The Sun God stands at the shore with an epic case of blue beach balls. He builds the Sun Temple and performs penance there. When we see the sexual positions carved into the walls of his temple we should understand her fear of being made a sex slave to this God. Chandrabhaga means tragic love." Dave smiles his ballroom smile.

Ascending Connecticut there's time to recall a sunny hillside rolling toward a blue harbor. I pull over with someone special sitting beside me. Replay a sled soaring down a mountainside of icepack and boulders. No one believed I missed that giant outcropping. Retrace a walk on the terraced footpath below the Spanish fort in St. Lucia. At the Honolulu zoo, my son chases birds and it upsets his little sister. My wife and kids snug in their beds, my brothers passed out on my couch. The chess set catches fireplace light so the pawns face off on a flaming battlefield. I'm newly divorced, currently unemployed and in route to the center square for Transcendentalism in America.

I'm embarrassed to admit the late date at which I became aware of the differences between a mineral, a stone and a gem. Over beer, I can expound on cement, concrete and paving stone. Tar, asphalt and blacktop are cousins. Resin, epoxy and block are roommates. There are differences among bhavana, sirpata and avatrana but in each case all heaven breaks loose.

The linga stone represents the male sex organ; a saucer (yoni) is his female counterpart. If your religion worships the joining of the two pass me an application. This subject has consumed man since he went to high school.

If you listen to the Hindus, a nameless God in the freezing loneliness of his Godhead seeks to amuse himself with a creation that will evolve to worship him. This is God's path to a self-realization he doesn't need. God's intention is unknowable for mortals. Assume that whatever else is going on isn't engaging him enough.

'The fastest way to improve your mood is to wash your floor."

A dark Israeli girl told me this. Her hair was smoke pouring off a burning oil tanker. I recall her advice because I'm worried about my mood. I need to get lost in this chore of driving to Carlisle. I'm not getting paid enough. I'm blocking out thoughts of being without a real job by recalling scenes from my India expedition. Reciting the poetry I wrote helps me get closer to my destination. I'm in a stare down with the road between where I am and where I need to be. When this is over, I'll wash my floors.

In the seventh century AD, the three original Hindu Gods, Brahma, Vishnu and Shiva are in danger of losing devotees to Buddhists and

Jains. The sixty-three Hindu poet-saints are commissioned to retell the story of creation in a way that the big three will enjoy resurgence. It amounts to a Crosby, Stills and Nash reunion tour, resulting in a renewed interest in the display of the linga. Driving two miles over the speed limit, I see myself a modern day poet-saint completing the sale of Shiva's icons to his temple in Carlisle.

. Shiva is the God we're concerned with in this travelogue. He is billed as the God of Destruction and displays four arms each holding a symbol. Behind his back the other Gods call him Swiss Army knife. He has a third eye he can weld with. With his arms outstretched he rides a white bull or a unicorn – a tribute to the starch in his linga. Other images of him have him stepping on a dwarf. Insatiable Shiva is arranged in marriage to the Goddess Shatki. She is a beauty who never uses the top half of her sari. With a ring in her nose and bells on her hands she sweeps Shiva into a porno double-feature.

Myth goes that she is getting slammed more times than a screen door and insists on having a baby to show for all the see-sawing in her yoni. Shiva wraps up a bundle of cloth and hands it to her.

"Here's a baby, Baby."

Shakti pulls the bundle to her breast and it springs to life a real baby. Sucking milk from one nipple causes the other to shoot a white line drive. This excites Shiva but Shakti pushes him away. She's busy feeding her baby. This enrages Shiva who uses his magic third eye to laser off the baby's head. Shakti screams so loud Shiva is afraid other Gods will interfere in his domestic bliss. He takes the head of a passing elephant calf and puts it on the baby's body. The baby with the elephant head is the God Ganesh, a symbol of good fortune for Hindus. He is known as the remover of all obstacles.

Shakti finds the little elephant face charming. Ganesh sits watching his parents screw and smiles his holy smile. He is often portrayed with his best friend, a rat. He is a lover of poetry.

From the beheading of the child we can see Shiva is a God of quick temper. He is also the God of Destruction in a religion that proposes that the sum total of the universe is constant. Everything destroyed gives rise to an equal creation. Besides being the Lord of Dance, Shiva is God of All Things that Live in Holes and Leader of All with No Place in Society

.

On this foggy Friday half-holiday only the chosen are at work. The rest of the world is clogging the mall entrances or at the movies. On opening day of the Christmas shopping season there's no excuse to be without a job. This bracelet on my wrist has turned me toward a $400 chore of body-guarding sacred stones. I'm a member of the transportation caste; my dharma is to oversee goods in transit.

The opening reel of Hindu creation stars the sea – the womb of the Hindu universe. On land Brahma seeks intercourse with his own daughter. She springs out of him a fully formed centerfold. His premature love drops spring to life as the Sages who create mankind – a population brought to life for the purpose of worshipping its Creator. When the earth is overrun with men aspiring to be God, Brahma fears heaven will be diluted. Gods will be a dime a deity if men can practice the self-discipline that attains divinity. In order to head this off, Brahma bestows a debasing order of senses on man. The urge to get laid is paramount among them. To make men earth-whipped, he invents women. Desire and jealousy become the cement shoes that bind man to the cycle of life and death. This is why women are evil to the hardcore Hindu. They stand in the way of men becoming God.   .

Hindus believe work is the worship of God. Thoreau suggests the less labor a man does the better off he will be. The original hippie of Concord says life is too short to be spent with our backs bent in forgettable chores. Thoreau would not have been attracted to sales. He didn't like listening as much as talking and was indifferent to grooming. He walked around in the woods rarely bathing and never dating. Imitating his lifestyle is an uphill climb.

.

I digress, as a man on a long drive is apt to do. Outside a Connecticut hamlet torn from Updike, I pass a wooden cross on the highway shoulder. It is encircled with flowers in vases and church candles. It reminds me of homes in India. The Ganesh elephant figurine is a favored knickknack in the Hindu household –popular as the Virgin Mary on the lawns of Staten Island.

The God Vishnu gets top billing in the famous Bhagahad Gita, the Bible of the Hindu religion. A comparable work on Shiva, the God we're concerned with in this class, is the Ramayana. A story in which he appears as a man called Rama.

In Dhunbad mosquitoes storm the house at twilight. The rooms must be flitted. Geeta and her older brother take John and me on a tour of town so the house is free to be crop-dusted. Geeta and I share the back seat with her two young nephews squeezed between us. John folds his giant frame into the front seat like a man entering a revolving door with skis on. His knees jut above the dashboard like twins in his lap. We drive past pitch black coalfields surrounding an occasional streetlamp. Crushed in back, I can smell Geeta's hair and see her eyes shine. She sings "Que sera, sera, whatever shall be shall be," and I slip down in my seat. Her nephews lead the applause when she finishes. Geeta smiles a smile that could jumpstart northeast India. I'm a snotty college kid, involved with a girl back home but tonight I'm in love with the modesty and charm of an Indian woman.

Thoreau was a bachelor and a virgin all his life. No wonder I didn't read his books. I can't cut through a vacant lot without imagining myself stumbling upon a woodland nymph. HDT immersed himself in nature and never did what comes naturally. He mooched off Emerson who was married so he must have seen how handy it was to have a woman on call. He was a grouchy old prude who bitched about the environment before it was actually screwed up. He was a Transcendentalist, a movement rooted in Hindu philosophy. It enjoyed a popularity in 1900s New England and then with the Beatniks in the 1950's. At no time did it suggest that you couldn't go out with girls. Gordon expounds on all this during our long rides through the Indian countryside. I'm fascinated by HDT's lack of sex – I'm bonding with the ascetic lifestyle.

"Bare feet predate shoes." This is the wiseass wisdom of Thoreau. We guess about how far into the woods he got before he put his boots back on

"Most men lead lives of quiet desperation." I'm driving another man's truck, chauffeuring icons to the temple of another man's God. A humble salesman, consumed with low intentions, I'm honored to take part in an errand whose aim is the worship of Shiva.

There are distinctions among a church, a cathedral and a temple. The dress code varies. You don't have to take off your shoes in church or cover your head. Wearing jeans and a Jets sweatshirt, I worry that I may insult the Hindu temple and offend the God of the Short Fuse.

Frank is the painter on our team. Five minutes after we lift off from JFK, he's telling me how much he's looking forward to getting laid in India. Frank's got whitened teeth and a George Hamilton tan. He's had two gallery shows in Long Island City while still in college. Over drinks, he tells me he's divorced and for some reason that makes me like him more. With his flashing smile, he seems a natural for hosting a game show. Frank will leave you mid-sentence if he gets a whiff of what he describes as "the triangle of life." We drink on the patio of the Bankipore Club. On the street a parade of maidens carry cargoes shaped as Easter bonnets.

Life burst from the body of Brahma. Certain castes came out of his knee, others from his thighs; demons jumped from his butt breathing fire, foretelling Indian cuisine. A white lily sprouted from his navel. From it emerged lesser Gods intent on battling demons. In the Greek style, Indian Gods love nothing better than setting forces at war with each other. Brahma was reckless enough to issue a boon to one demon named Ravana. The boon protected the demon from censure by any God. When Ravana made himself a great nuisance to creation, Brahma created a mortal to tone him down. The man's name was Rama and he was the manifestation of Shiva in human form. The Hindu text Ramayana is the tale of Rama going toe to toe with Ravana after the demon kidnaps his wife. Film at 11.

"A man is rich in terms of what he can do without," Thoreau suggests in Walden Pond. This book was assigned in high school but I never read it. HDT trooped around Carlisle many times in his short life. He read and admired the Hindu texts when he wasn't skipping rocks in the pond. By solitude and fasting, he evoked the mood of India. He dined on rice balls.

HDT theorized that "a man can date a new era in his life from the reading of a book." Walden was that book for Gordon. He read it in high school and it set him off walking the trails of upstate New York. When he started his study of nature, he joined the New York State Horticulture Society. By hanging around its West 58th St. headquarters, he was assigned a position. Gordon was a star student and was pursued by gardening magazines upon his college graduation. He stayed at St. John's and taught American literature. When he agreed to lead our trip to India, it was because he wanted to spread the gospel of a man he considered an American mystic. A natural leader and diplomat, Gordon is also a decorated Rotarian.

Paul Harris started the Rotary in Chicago back when men wore spats. He and two business associates got into a routine of having lunch together once a week. They moved from one restaurant to another so the name Rotary made sense. Soon they began sticking their noses into local charities. Along with getting out of the office, doing good works made them feel good. From this humble beginning, Rotary has spread to every corner of the world. It is no longer required that clubs change restaurants weekly. Be assured that in any hamlet you stumble into there is a club of businessmen eating lunch in a sensible restaurant on a weekday. There is a Rotary Club of Carlisle and a Rotary Club of Bokaro Steel City. After the passing of Paul Harris, the very room where he and his cohorts conceived of the Rotary Club was disassembled and reassembled on the seventeenth floor of the world headquarters of Rotary International in Flint, Michigan - a vacation stop you might threaten your kids with.

Dharma is a code of behavior that every Hindu aspires to. Its recipe is as precise as the Big Mac. Worship, sacrifice, and work for the glory of God in the vocation assigned you. In everything you do, ask divine assistance. Back when we were whistle-stopping Bihar on our Rotary-sponsored student exchange, I considered myself a poet. Back home, I find the only enterprise that rewards daily self-examination is sales. Munching at Mickey D's, I ask myself, "Would I be better off as an unsuccessful poet or an unsuccessful salesman?"

Yesterday was Thanksgiving; I had turkey, clams, and beer at my sister's house. I shouldn't be hungry but the number of McDonald's that have been allowed to settle on I-95 in Connecticut has overcome me. Like a bee on a hive, I attach myself to a seat and eat while staring at the menu board where I imagine what else I might have ordered.

India is a nation of salespeople. Westerners can't walk around without drawing a flock of hawkers. Men thin as swizzle sticks wave wares in your face as if to hypnotize. When my mates and I hit Delhi, we get chased around like the Beatles in Help. Everyone has something to sell. I write a poem about the street vendors who dog us as paparazzi.

pay to see a cobra fight a mongoose

or watch a man levitate

at the wall of the Red Fort

a good price for inlaid jewelry boxes

and a studded leather whip

what will you pay for this string of slides?

shots of the Taj at twilight

consider these lead figurines

depicting the sexual positions

for you Sahib, guess how many rupees?

There is polite applause and I see Gordon touch his brow. Each time I get up I see my team squirm in their seats. Reading poetry aloud puts people on edge.

Poetry is the woven basket no one wants to buy. After returning from India, I compile a collection of what I've written while we were on tour. I mail copies to three publishers in Delhi and one to Rotary International. Acknowledgement of receipt is still pending. As an afterthought I decide a cover letter might have been helpful. The original copy is filed in my work desk. I vow to revisit them if I'm ever wrapped in a body cast.

On a long drive like this one, if you intend to mull something over it takes awhile to get into the adult swim hour of mulling. Trading Connecticut for Rhode Island, I've yet to settle on an explanation for the missing crate. I've been distracted by a hamburger chain, India home movies and regrets sharp enough to make me smack my steering wheel.

At the Rotary adopted village of Ullgora, we get our first look at Chhau dancing. Dave takes the seat of honor next to the village chief. People seem to think Dave has published a book on Chhau. He's only done a term paper. I have no interest in diminishing his accomplishments but people are calling him "Doctor" and he's not correcting them. When the dancing starts, you can't tell one number from another. Randy sits immersed in the ritual. I see Frank looking around wondering if he can get away with smoking a Marlboro. If he takes out American cigarettes it will create a stampede of grubbers. Gordon and I sit flirting with the children. After the program ends, we blow up Rotary balloons and hand them to village kids. The chief invites us on a walking tour of his village. We snap pictures and ask stupid questions. On the west side of the village, a Rotary Eye Bank does cataract operations three days each month. A crowd of teenagers follows us and while everyone else sits for tea, I play grapple with a young man who flips me over his hip to the delight of his friends. It's all good fun. I get in the car thankful I haven't had to use the village latrine.

Stay with me, Brahma is King of the Universe and Shiva is the middle brother on Bonanza. While in India, I spend my evenings talking to beautiful Hindu women but not about the Gods they worship. Most Indian homes have a small altar with a wallet-sized photo of their favored Guru. I don't remember ever seeing a linga during my college tour. They can be small as a salt shaker or large as a dinosaur egg. They are displayed upright, balanced on a saucer. The saucer (yoni) invokes the female sexual organ; as if sex was balancing your penis on a plate.

I didn't pay any attention to Shiva while in India. Dave talked of the Lord of Dance but I didn't recall it until Surrinder reminded me. I knew very little about Thoreau until Gordon brainwashed me. Now Shiva's stones tap my shoulder every time I touch the brakes. I'm on the way to the deep woods of Thoreau.

Find here the Cliff notes on Ramayana. It is a roman de clef on the God Shiva. A great King has no sons. He pleads with the Gods and they give him four sons by three wives. The youngest wife bestows her charms on the King with such effect that he promises her that her son will take the throne after his death. The King summons his oldest son Rama and tells him his birthright belongs to his younger brother. Rama with his wife Sita and another brother go into exile. This injustice suggests a source of Shiva's wicked temper.

While hunting in a magic forest, Rama is approached by a demon princess who eyes his linga. "Drop that stick of straw you're married to." Her robe opens to reveal breasts upturned as peppers.

"Be gone she-devil." Rama's linga stirs despite his refusal.

Pissed at being dismissed, the she-devil sends her brother to kick Rama's ass. Rama slays the brother and his army of flying monkeys. Now the princess's Dad gets involved. His name is Ravana, the Demon King of Lanka. He tells his daughter to disguise herself as a deer and lure Rama's brother away from body-guarding Rama's wife Sati. Rama is out of town when his brother chases after the whitetail. Sati is kidnapped and carried across the sea to the Evil Kingdom. Pass the popcorn.

Stripped naked and tied to a café chair, Sati is a Hindu Pauline. Her breasts swell around her restraints. Ravana puts a hand on her ass but can go no further. Long ago he raped a woman owned by a God. A spell was cast on him that makes it impossible for him to take a woman by force. Sita is safe from his linga.

Ravanna attempts to seduce Sati with a dozen hand maidens to do her wash. She is shown a kingdom and a hall of jeweled saris all her size. If she gives herself to him, she will know true bliss. She closes her eyes and prays her husband will rescue her.

Jaw firm as Flash Gordon, Rama speeds across the sky with his own monkey air force. They open a can of ass whip on the Evil Kingdom that trickles down to the lowest paid extra. Ravanna flees as he senses Rama is the God Shiva in human form. Rama takes a long look at Sati before untying her.

Chapter Two. News of his victory over Ravanna results in Rama being invited to a nearby kingdom where he is challenged to bend a bow that no man has been able to string. Rama runs his hands over it as if making love to a beautiful woman. He whispers and rubs the length of it against his linga. Sap runs the length of the bow.

"Is he going to bow it or …" the people's question goes unasked. The string closes over the open end of the bow; now curved as a hula hoop. Every arrow shot from the bow turns to gold.

In return for this feat, Rama is given the Princess Uma, fourteen and ripe as a Jersey tomato. "Bend me as you wish, beautiful Master." The apron of Uma's sari is wet.

Sita is having none of that. She reaches into her husband's lungi. She is enflamed from being tied up. Her name means "furrow." "The mongoose awaits the cobra." She reveals a glistening yoni topped by a pearl centered as a beeti.

"Mama Mia" (or something to that effect) Rama says and then takes his wife, Uma and his flying monkeys back to his forest lair. No mortal can keep two wives under the same roof and Rama is no exception. He questions Sita about her time as prisoner of the Demon King. She is disgraced by his implications. She reminds Rama of how close he held her on the night of her rescue.

"Did you smell another man on me?"

"Since you brought it up."

Sita throws herself onto a burning ghat because her husband doubts her virtue. There is no excuse for a Hindu woman being anywhere other than by her husband's side. This begins the rite of "sati" where a widow is expected to embrace the flaming corpse of her husband. Sita's self-immolation foretells the practice. Uma takes over the sexual chores for Rama and his brother. She's a younger woman after all.

The Ramayana stresses the dharma of honoring your spouse. The wife has no life outside her husband. If you were to recklessly open books and start reading, you might encounter a version of the Ramayana that differs from what we have here. I'm giving you the story as it was told to me or how I remember it being told to me back on that Ganges spring break. One of my hosts suggested a book of poems retelling the Ramayana – I have spared you that.

I get into poetry to meet girls. Also it's easier to write without having to make sense. College is awash with poetesses. My first day of class, I meet a girl who spent a summer in an iron lung. Another writes a poem to her breasts. I start writing about famous prisoners like Robert Stroud and Al Capone; the Alcatraz breakouts and death row folklore. A slender young classmate in a peasant blouse and designer jeans asks me if I was ever incarcerated. Incarcerated is a poem all on its own. I turn away; as if by answering a wound might reopen. We end up kissing in the shadows of the Rathskeller.

My college tour passes through Surrinder's hometown, Bokaro Steel City. I meet him twenty years later; he mentions the place and I declare myself a homie. We had dinner in Bokaro with Russian engineers on loan to India's steel industry. Doing shots of cognac, we talk through an interpreter who looks like the collection basket man at my Polish parish. I'm too drunk to be embarrassed by my sentimental toast to our parents. We're a long way from home and in no shape to drink with Russians. Frank blurts out something in Ukrainian – who knew that was even a language? One engineer is from the same town as Frank's grandma. This calls for two more toasts.

Out the back window of Surrinder's truck, the lingas in the cargo bed rock in their crates like warheads. I'm three and a half hours into this ride and passing through a stretch of I-95 that passes below wooden row houses. There is no reason for me to race; I haven't figured out what to say when I arrive.

I write poems on the long drives between towns. At each Rotary Club function we're expected to sing the National Anthem and give a short bio of ourselves. John and Randy are seasoned performers. Dave always finds something to say. Frank flashes his teeth and I read a poem about the day's activities.

In the tradition of Vasco De Gama, Frank arrives in India intent on fornication. He suggests it is the primary way to immerse oneself in a foreign culture. "An artist is concerned with how people make love."

"What makes you say that, Frank?" On long drives I tend to challenge remarks to pass time.

"The artist is a man of action. Do you know who said that?"

"Joseph Conrad," Frank answers his own question.

"I loved him on Ironsides." I offer.

Frank doesn't pause.

"Lovemaking uses all the arts, dance, drama, poetry, music all for the pleasure of an audience of one."

"How does painting fit in?" I ask.

Frank makes a motion suggesting his linga is a paintbrush.

Tantric Hinduism as explained by Dave is a practical path to supernatural power. The more I hear of it, the more it appears our best chance of getting laid in India. The Tantric student uses his lower impulses for higher aims. He seeks God through the pursuit of things that guys love to do. The Vaisnava Sahajiyas are a tantric Hindu cult that

124

worships the goddess Shakti. They consider sexual union with her the stepping off point for attaining Godhead – no pressure.

When Brahma took a poke at the female that sprang from his loins, he was joining the male and female sides of his own divinity. This coupling resulted in sakipata (descent of divine energy to earth). Tantric disciples hope to ascend to heaven through their worship of the sex act. They meet in social clubs to worship the yoni of the goddess Shakti. They drink, smoke and screw. At times they practice cakrapuja which is a sexual break dance. Puja is the word for worship; cakra – do the vocabulary. An ideal tantric disciple adept in the act of intercourse withholds his ejaculation and turns that energy back into his own body. This provides him a supernatural power he will need to get to sleep.

When I won the poetry contest and went to India, I began morphing into sales. Seven weeks of public speaking and poetry reading to audiences who didn't understand either was my sales boot camp. For the next twenty years I've changed jobs like other guys change cars, but always I've kept my positive outlook. Then my wife fired me.

A perfect pitch isn't seen. Salesmanship is making people perceive that doing business with you elevates them. Why they care about you and your product is where you come in; it's why they pay you. Regardless of my story, we're not getting anywhere if you think I'm full of crap. That's a phrase too often associated with sales. When I reach Carlisle, I don't want to come off like I'm hauling fertilizer.

I may begin by touching on the journey that brought the lingas from Patna to Port Newark – a salad before entrée. I'll proclaim it a miracle that they ever made it this far by underlining the corruption and red tape Surrinder had to navigate. Let the missing fifth case surface in the light of how lucky we are to have these four. A theory that the fifth case (full of bogus stones) was used to pay off a corrupt official can be suggested without providing actual detail. The happy ending is that every linga that left India is now in Carlisle. That's my story and I'm sticking to it – a white collar lie to devotees of a brown God.

Four hours into my drive, tedium has me in a rear naked choke. The rain and fog have erased the scenery. I wouldn't say traffic is light. I haven't turned the radio on because I'm forcing myself to rehearse a story. Hugging the wheel, I remind myself to look before changing lanes.

The purpose of life is to become aware of the divine. That's Hinduism in a betel nutshell. Many Gods make for many ways to approach the one God who is all things at all times. Shiva is the God in our batter's box and he holds many sacred batting titles.

Brahma, Vishnu, and Shiva mirror the Father, Son and Holy Ghost. Avatarana is the descent of the Divine into the world. I drive around believing my God walked this earth and the Hindus believe their God's walked it before him. We have that much in common. We don't pray as

126

much as the Hindus so they may be in closer touch with their creator. Jesus walked the earth two thousand years and change ago. On a Hindu calendar that's the time it takes a star to blink.

Abhimukti is escaping the cycle of life and death. Hindus pray they be excused from reincarnation. The hopeful part of this life is that if we live it well, we're one turn closer to the end of the merry-go-round. When you see God in swirling water and divinity in moving foliage, you're assumed to be making progress.

any Howard Beach car park

boasts a nobler rig

than our Ganges water taxi

cruising the River of Life

we drink tea from clay cups

throw the empties over the side

snap photos as we putt putt past

crowds of faithful bathers

I'm from the old school of sales. I call a man Mr. until he tells me not to. I've got a thousand miles on my shoes but they're shined. I can make you like me. I'm not a phony but honesty is a coin I spend sparingly. I chase a commission check. I'm a salesman unashamed. If I walk around with my fly open, I'm better off having stayed in bed. First impressions last. I carry a quality pen to leave behind and a business card that radiates efficiency. I always walk out backwards so the last thing my client sees is my smile. I won't leave without a firm appointment to revisit. You don't need a Harvard degree to do this stuff. It doesn't take talent to run out a groundball.

Toilet tissue was an issue for our group. We were supposed to be focused on deeper concerns. One afternoon in a small town library, John began his address to the congregation with an apology. "I hope no one ever needs the pages headed ETHOPIA and ETRUSCAN from your encyclopedia." Another night at a formal dinner, Frank gets up wearing a white shirt under his Rotary blazer. "Let me explain what happened to my tie."

Entering Massachusetts, I'm reminding myself to act naturally; use limited responsibility (I'm just a driver) while insisting on my fee. I'll need coffee so it will be nice if it is offered. A tip wouldn't be turned down. I have no fund for unplanned expenses – the cash is for my daughter's self-defense pajamas.

Zoomorphic deities are a part of the Hindu religion. Catholics don't ascribe spiritual powers to animals. Far as I know, Jesus didn't even have a cat. The Hindus worship elephants, cows, snakes and rats. Their Gods assume these lower forms to test the kindness of men. The Jains consider all life sacred and wear surgical masks to avoid breathing in a mosquito.

We are guests of a Jain in Ramapur. He serves us eggs. Jains don't bury their dead but set corpses on outside altars to be picked at by birds. On their road to their next reincarnation, they take a turn as a salad bar. Jains have an aversion to onions.

Thoreau once translated a text called The Transmigration of Seven Brahmans and then shoved it in a drawer. He opted for Civil Disobedience and who can question his marketing savvy? In India a holy man is often supported by the society around him. People will feed a Swami aspiring to be divine - up in New England, not so fast. Thoreau chose to spend time daydreaming beside a pond but that did not entitle him to dip his spoon in the community clam chowder. Like me, Thoreau was expected to produce revenue. Today I'm driving on the Path of Renunciation where I'm performing a time-consuming task for a minimum wage. I offer this effort to the God Shiva; to him I pray, to him I dedicate this holy errand.

Shiva is the first man. As with Adam he occupies a lush garden, sitting beneath a tree of knowledge, Shiva's mind trips around the universe in contemplation of the unknowable God whose name men can't agree on. While sitting with his hair uncombed, Shiva's linga springs to life. It symbolizes his desire to evolve. Devi, Mother of Creation while looking down from heaven, spots Shiva and his woody. Devi manifests herself in the form of Sati, a Hindu centerfold. Dark hair, cinnamon skin and breasts swirled as butterscotch servings make her a Bollywood adult film star. Shiva gets to his feet and starts marching behind his linga. He sweeps Sati away to a mountain top where they invent sex in all its forms and practices. When Sati dies (fatigue?), Shiva walks the earth with his linga dragging in the dust. Other Gods complain that all of creation is being buzz-killed by Shiva's epic bad mood.

In an effort to restore his humor, they reincarnate Sati as Parvati but call her Shakti. She is a younger model of Sati with goose eggs on her odometer. Her perfumed garden, love sleeve, her delta of Venus brings to life Shiva's linga. Together they create the Kama Sutra. Their lovemaking rattles cosmic knickknacks. From the heat of their joining, "chakras" are sent spinning on the earth. They are the invisible whirlwinds we call the arts. Music, astrology, massage, painting, dance, poetry and drama become avenues through which man can approach God.

"Beware of enterprises that require new clothes." This is one of Gordon's Thoreauisms. I'm wearing my red Rotary blazer. We are guests of Vinny Kocher under his party tent on the roof of his icehouse. It is our welcoming dinner party. I'm envisioning beautiful women charmed by my New York accent. My tie clip is a Rotary wheel and my lapel pin an American flag.

"What is the aim of man?" Randy asks.

"Women," Frank and I chime in unison. We are surveying a cocktail hour bathed in torchlight. We disperse into the crowd as pick-pockets.

With your indulgence, a last Shiva yarn from the Hindu highlight reel. If his press is true, Shiva makes Mick Jagger look like a monk and Yogi Berra a guy with nothing to say. On page one of creation, Brahma and Vishnu are arguing over who will have the greatest influence over the earth. From nowhere a giant penis extends across the sky. Its beginning and end are beyond the vision of the Gods. Brahma turns himself into a goose and flies off to find the tip. Vishnu turns himself into a boar and digs into the earth in search of the root. Unable to measure the dimensions, they return exhausted. A vagina opens on the side of the penis and out of it Shiva drops down to earth, his hair a mop head of black mambas.

Brahma and Vishnu recognize him as a power not to be dismissed. They welcome him as the hat trick of a Hindu Godhead. Shiva takes charge of the destruction of things, Vishnu is the preserver of things, and Brahma keeps them apart. The three Gods stand staring up at the sky-wide penis throbbing with power outside time.

. One way to pass time on a long drive is to consider the relationship of God and nature. Thoreau suggests that because God is so obvious he is invisible. Nature is God's floor plan. Trees pray with upraised arms as an example for men. If a man finds answers in the world around him, why does he insist on looking inside himself? The Hindu word "ajnana" means "I do not know that I am God." We create the universe that is the setting for our self-realization. There is no reason to look inside ourselves because we are never outside ourselves.

Thoreau suggests that union with God can only be achieved by personal effort. By seeking God, I become God – echoes of the Guru's words when I asked him to define poetry. Straightening that concept out helps snap me back from the waking sleep of long driving.

At a highway gas stop, I pick up a hitchhiker with a Santa beard. His black watch cap is pulled down over dirty hair. Wearing a black poncho, he appears to be dressed in a garbage bag. I'm hoping this coot will have an idea about where I'm headed.

"Where ya headed, boss?" It's a ghetto affectation to call old white men boss. When he gets in the car, I see his poncho is a garbage bag.

"North," he sounds like he's taking a guess.

"Off we go." I swing back onto the highway. Ten minutes later he hasn't said a word or taken his eyes off the road. It occurs to me I may be in company of a mental patient.

"Are you military?" This is the most ridiculous question I can think of. The guy looks like a bridge troll.

"Nope."

"Lots of service guys hitch up here from New York." I'm pulling this out of my ass. I have no evidence for anything I'm saying.

"I wouldn't know that." It's closer to a full sentence.

"How long were you standing there?" As a salesman, I'm obliged to carry the conversation.

"I pump gas at that stop on the overnight. I've been standing as long as I can remember."

"No easy money having to stand." I'm suggesting I have personal experience that I don't.

"The less work a man does the better off he is."

"Your old lady must love hearing that."

"Don't have an old lady."

"Bragging or complaining?"

"Bragging."

I wait for him to ask me if I'm married. The road swims over the hood and across the windshield.

"I'm going to Carlisle. Have you ever been there?"

"Yup."

"You'll help me with directions?"

"Yup."

I take a break from trying to get this guy to talk. I smell gas and body odor. To cover the sound of me cracking the window, I ask,

"Do you drive?"

"Nope."

"It would cut down on a lot of unnecessary conversation if you did." I'm spraining my sarcastic.

"If I seem obtuse, I apologize." He continues staring straight ahead. I consider that word 'obtuse'. I didn't expect that. His profile inspires a haymaker.

"Has anyone ever told you that you look like Thoreau?"

"Nope."

I elect to get metaphysical. "How best does man approach God?"

"In silence."

It is starting to rain. I move my wipers from OFF to INTERMITTENT

.

I shake the hand of Sister Mary Francis

her cloud white habit

whiter against the mud walls

of the Mother of India Hospital

on a narrow bed a woman recovers

from a self-induced abortion

she's been exiled by her village

into the hands of the Catholic Sisters

Randy demands the young nun answer

for the Vatican's lack of support

she scolds him with her smile

135

"Many others need much more than we."

palm branches wipe our windshield

the departure creates a dust cloud

our nun ascends above it

waving at us as we wave back

Gordon's avocation is horticulture. He has a Masters in American literature from Hofstra and knows more about Thoreau than I consider reasonable. He's an assistant dean at St. John's who can talk fauna and HDT at the same sitting. I should get college credits for riding around with him. He's surprised that I don't know Thoreau's poetry. I never finished Walden and I suspect I'm not alone.

Gordon has the grace of a natural leader. Team members complain to him and he listens with the sincerity of a salesman. He resists the impulse to act, an enlightened approach in a situation where addressing one complaint gives birth to another. He is used to being around college brats and doesn't give a crap if we're uncomfortable.

We fly from Patna to Ranchi. Water buffalo patrol the airstrip where we land. Ranchi is an emerging suburb sprung from a long established village. I am the guest of a man who owns a sari shop. I fall in love with his kids. With my Etch A Sketch I draw, fish, birds, and elephants. They seem to think I'm going to leave the toy when I go. We cry and wave and promise letters. Randy proposes that every person we meet in life is a letter from God.

"You're junk mail," Frank cracks. Randy's divinity is without chink. He will not be baited. Jokes and sarcastic jabs pass through him like swords through a magician's assistant.

Randy is a minister in a Protestant congregation impossible to pronounce. It starts with espies, veers into univocal and soars over a cliff with tents. He gave me his card but I can't find it. In his spare time Randy runs a theater workshop at the Flushing Y. It allows teens to act out gangsta emotions. He holds a Master of Divinity degree from the New Brunswick Theological Seminary of the Reformed Church of America. Every time Gordon uses that title to introduce Randy, I expect him to swallow his tongue.

"Is there a Master of Divinity in the house?" I like to call this out when dinner conversation devolves into complaints about road travel. We often rate each other's after dinner speeches. Over nightcaps we solve the problems of India. Agreed upon by all of us is that getting to places on time is not part of Indian culture. We often sit waiting for drivers who arrive late and a car short. They race us through a score of whistle stops. We are ambassadors packed into Ambassadors.

At lunch in a garden ringed with bougainvillea, the breeze is a little girl's smile.

"Are we not men?" I toast my crew with double Seven.

"Reform begins with the perfection of the individual." Randy says this with a straight face. We get whiplash from the conversation braking. Frank signals our waiter.

"Can I get mine to go?"

"I paraphrase the great Henry David Thoreau when I say that the most encouraging fact of life is that we can improve ourselves if we choose to. My team and I have traveled around the world to meet with you, share this meal, and be improved by this experience. Our visit today is a ripple on the ocean. Over time it will change the relationship between the United States and India."

Gordon's opening remarks never stray far from this recipe: a reference to Thoreau, a nod to our hosts, then the suggestion that our cultural exchange will benefit the world outside our window. This is followed by the introduction of team members.

Gordon likes John to lead off because he's tall and seems taller when he's the only one standing. Dave, Frank and I are place setters. Randy speaks clean up because everything he says sounds torn from the New Testament.

I steer into the afternoon sun. Silent Sam riding shotgun remains mum. I'm not saying anything until he says something to me. I could turn the radio on but that might serve as his excuse for not speaking. He's my guest shouldn't he at least toss up some small talk? Am I obliged to entertain him and drive? I'm recalling a poem I wrote while lying on a rope bed in Dr. Mehta's garden.

Sputa Das Gupta aka Spice Eyes

follows me to the Sun Temple

sex queens in stone wink at me

I hear her name on the breeze

she slipped into my bed last night

slender as a Nepalese Keno Queen

stamped my passport and visa

now my shadow takes her shape

It's all fantasy. I can't get arrested anywhere in northeast India. I'm falling in love with Indian women at every stop without every getting one in un-chaperoned company. Rolls of midsection, child bearing hips, kohl eyes, and glittering beetis make them appear circus queens. Sex-obsessed mythology, a world of babies, the hometown of the Kama Sutra, and I'm getting nothing but cold showers. I ask forgiveness for my earthbound interests but it is the man I am in person.

"Reduce your affairs to two or three rather than a hundred or a thousand," Thoreau advised. My concerns are that the truck is running good and I have a sense of what to say when I reach Carlisle. Without limiting myself to an actual script, I have a tale that suggests an explanation. My drive time is acceptable. The hitchhiker is insurance against getting lost. All I have to do is "Stride confidently in the direction of my dreams."

There is no college for sales. It's a field you wind up in if you're good at nothing else. Salespeople are the happiest-acting mother-fathers in the working world. They are out visiting people while the staff eyes the clock from rat maze cubicles. The rest of us can be replaced by a cheaper version of ourselves but you don't trifle with the rainmaker. If it wasn't for him you might have to go out and find new business. Today I'm charged with delivering four crates to a client who has paid for five. Its sales work.

People hate salespeople because sometime in their life they've been one on one with one. Looking into the eyes of some wound up swinging dick selling cardboard inserts is worst than sitting next to a poet at a cocktail party. You don't want to hear his shit. Life is too fucking short. I apologize for the language but there is a passionate resistance to sales that can't be understated. It's why we get paid. In India I was a poet but I'm going to Carlisle as a salesman. It's the difference between art and artifice.

Another Hindu slant on creation; then I swear no more. The God Parapet a.k.a. Brahma is in bed with his own daughter. Other Gods disapprove but no one has the balls to stop it. They enlist the demon Radar to put an end to the non-stop incest. Radar shoots an arrow into Parapet's heart. The copulating stops, as the two lovers fall away from each other, a stallion springs from him and a mare from her. They are followed by a ram and a ewe, a rooster and a chicken, a Mr. and Mrs. Goldfish--basically the cast of Noah's ark. As reward for his shot that populates the animal world, Radar is given lordship over cows. Cows are the all-star species of the Hindus. They won't eat them or even shoo them away. Cows graze in public parks, eating lawns and hedges. They are worshipped in a country where there is not enough meat. It evokes the brilliance of Gandhi. He got India fed by going on a hunger strike.

"Mind if I smoke?" I'm pulled back to the present by his question. My hitchhiker has spoken. "Okay if I smoke?" Now he's said it twice.

"It's not my truck but if you bring the window down it shouldn't be a problem." I note his smoker's teeth,

"Thanks." He pulls a hand-rolled cigarette from inside his parka. It's crooked as a witch's finger.

"Out of store bought?" I ask.

141

He flicks a Bic and puffs. I catch a whiff that carries me back to Bihar. He's smoking bidi. Without turning my head, I think I see out the corner of my eye, him holding the cigarette and the lighter with two right hands.

Thoreau would smack me on the back of the head for doing this drive. To him, a man should be busy giving thanks he's not a pack animal. Time- consuming chores distract us from the self-realization that is our purpose on earth. Nature is God winking at man. Everyone is a self-published guide to their own divinity. In reading himself, a man comes to know his purpose. These are the post it notes for transcendentalism.

Tandava is Shiva's greatest dance. It originated at the dawn of time. Shiva dances to celebrate the destruction of darkness and ignorance. He dances at the thought of making love to a woman. He dances in the ashes of the dead. Finally, he dances for no reason. I make these notes from Dave's discourse on what we've seen at Ullgora.

In Jamshedpur we are guests of the Rotary at Baldih House. Unfolding ourselves from a seventy mile car ride, our hosts greet us with red and white garlands. Inside we look to find a drink. "Tandi" means cold and we say it to anyone who appears to be a bartender. Served big bottles of good beer that could be colder, we smile and shake hands. People want their picture taken with John and he arches his eyebrows to show his good humor. We eat from tables marked VEG and NON-VEG. By now we're old hands at spotting a curry IED in a plate of gupta. When finished, we put our plates under the table. This afternoon we will meet with the Tagore Society. I'm expected to read some poems in memory of India's greatest poet. After that we tour the Tata Steel factory and the Telco truck plant. No sense resisting these visits; Rotarians insist we pay our respects to the industries of India, major sponsors of local arts.

"That's a bidi, isn't it Mate?" I'm feeling lightheaded from my first whiff of second hand smoke.

"Yes." He doesn't offer me one.

"No thanks, I'm getting plenty just sitting here."

He has rolled his window down halfway. The cabin of the truck is smoky as a rock concert.

"Carlisle is approached via a series of right turns beginning with the exit after this one." Suddenly I'm getting the Gettysburg address from this guy. I've forgotten I don't know where I'm going.

"Thanks."

Now I'm short on words. I know Shiva carries his four arms at right angles. Hindu art abounds in 90 degree angles. It suggests divinity cannot be approached directly. The swastika was born in India. Frank's discourse on this subject comes to mind twenty years after I first heard it. It surfaces like the lyrics of an oldie.

"Where do you go to buy bidi?" As a salesman I'm obligated to collect information.

"My boss smokes them."

Emboldened by a contact high, I can't shut up.

"I went to India my junior year in college. I smoked bidi, chewed betel nut, and ate balls of cannabis. I partook of hashish and pan spiked with opiate. I threw up at the Taj Mahal. I'm sorry I didn't get your name."

"Steve."

"Steve, I hope you don't take offense but you're not really carrying your side of this conversation. Let me suggest you don't have a woman because you have to talk to one before they agree to get near you. Tell me to shut up if you think it's none of my business."

"I see you value speech."

"I'm a salesman, mate. If I don't talk, I don't eat. Having nothing to say, we might as well be water buffalo. I have a feeling you don't agree."

"We just passed our exit." He smiles a betel nut red smile.

I realize I've been rattling. I might have stopped talking in the middle of a sentence.

Many successful people will admit over a drink that they can't do sales. They can administrate, delegate, regulate and initiate but can't talk anybody into buying anything. Responsibilities don't scare them but having to knock on a door makes their knees weak. It is the chore of breaking down buyer resistance that people reject. It's human nature not to pressure someone into doing something. It flies in the face of the way your Mother brought you up.

"Can I get off the next exit and backtrack?" I'm embarrassed at having lost track of where we're going.

"Carlisle is approached by a series of right turns."

"Again? I'll take that as a yes?" Something about my guest is making me nervous. As a sales professional, I'm charged with establishing rapport with everyone I meet.

"As you say it, do it," he adds. Great, he's stoned on his ass.

"I'm getting off. Just direct me."

"Of course," we're back to two-word sentences.

Rotary Clubs, Lions Clubs and Chambers of Commerce gravitate to affordable neighborhood restaurants. Lunch meetings can range from acceptable company to watching pipe rust. Rotarians are civic-minded businessmen who devote money and energy to the common good. They adopt causes and drive their spouses to tears supporting them. If you are a start-up lawyer or a CPA, the Rotary Club is a great place to network. If you're retired and your wife wants you out of the house, Rotary welcomes you with open arms. I've spent more time in the Rotary Clubs of India than anywhere else. The first restaurant we pass, once off the highway, is home to the Rotary Club of Carlisle. Let's call it a good luck stop. I need to pee and drink a beer.

Geeta, sweet amiga

a blown glass wind chime

you sing so I can't breathe

in the backseat of Dad's Ambassador

the gas lamps of Dhunbad

flare inside your eyes

Whatever Shall Be Shall Be

you perform for a festival of coal fields

The people at the Tagore Center give me polite applause. I suspect they expect more passion and a young man to boast about his homeland.

146

I give them love letters in poems shorter than what they are used to. They appear caught off-guard by the brevity of my presentation. Regardless of what you do in poetry, people will give you a pass. No matter how good your poems are their favorite part is when they end

Behind the restaurant, the Concord River curls like smoke from the busboy's cigarette. Atop the bar there are photos showing the river frozen over, men ice-fishing, kids ice-skating, and snowmobilers spraying snow. Its Friday after Thanksgiving and the river has yet to freeze. On the bank, a wrecked Dodge awaits colder weather. Once it is pulled out on the ice, it becomes the subject of a pool - picking the spring day when the car becomes a submarine.

The bar is dark and quiet enough to inspire drinking. Conversation moves like a shadow. You can get up, go pee, and then sit back down in the pauses men take between exchanges about the weather. I try the pay phone but get no answer from the number Surrinder has given me. On a bulletin board, a notice advises that the town paper will be not be publishing for the next two weeks- the editor is on vacation.

Steve the sphinx, on a corner barstool, keeps one hand on his beer glass as if afraid it will walk off. He stares straight ahead intent as an iguana. A bartender's nightmare, Steve can make eight ounces of Bud last three innings.

"No answer," I announce, as if someone was waiting to hear about the outcome.

"I'm looking for the Shiva Temple in Carlisle," I ask the bartender with the white hair and western vest. He stares at me so long I'm uncertain he understands English.

"I expect you'll have no problem."

"Why?"

"You're drinking with the guy who owns the place."

A private room on the side of the bar must be where they conduct Rotary meetings. There's a cogwheel banner on the wall above a long table lined with empty chairs.

John was an orphan in Norway. His parents adopted him and brought him to the States. He turned out to be worth the expense. As an only child he was coddled. He began playing music as a preschooler and grew to master a grocery list of instruments. He breezed through academics, often tutoring kids a grade or two ahead of him. By fifth grade, it was clear he would be the tallest kid in any class he took. Coaches scolded John for not playing sports. He hated games, especially basketball. He didn't mind wearing a costume and banging a drum so he became the last kid in line for the marching band. John was used to being stared at but the attention he generated in India was unprecedented. Kids chased him as if a giraffe was loose on Main Street.

.

Back in the truck, I'm tearing Silent Steve a new one.

"What are you trying to pull?"

"Nothing."

"Why didn't you say something, Pops? I've been trying to talk to you for over an hour. Are you going to pay me for these goddamn stones?"

"There not all here."

"What makes you say that?"

"There's a case missing."

"Damn straight there's a case missing and for a good goddamn reason." In sales never play defense. We sit in silence for five full minutes; neither one of us wants to be the next to speak.

"You know so much, I'm sure you know what happened to the missing case." I lose the "don't speak" duel.

"Refresh me." He gestures for me to make a left with his left hand then to veer right with his right hand meanwhile he's holding a beer with another hand in his lap. I bought him one for the road. I didn't want to wait for him to drink it at the bar; it's getting dark.

"I'm not sure how you're doing that trick with the extra hands and I'm not sure I want to know." Now I'm avoiding eye contact.

A dirt driveway slopes down to a gravel car park. There's a bread loaf mailbox with a statue of Shiva welded on top as a hood ornament. The house is a bastard mother-daughter undergoing construction. On the stoop stands a linga the size of a birdhouse gourd. Upstairs I'm steered into an easy chair. My host disappears into an adjoining room and returns dressed in the traditional Gandhi diaper with over the shoulder shawl. I now see clearly four arms, two on each side of his body. On his forehead he wears a beeti the size of a poker chip.

"You're the God Shiva." I'm not as slow as I seem.

"We'll get to that. I apologize for not speaking in the car but I had to know more about you. You'll have many questions but we don't have much time."

"Yes, I'm anxious to leave as well."

"Have you ever heard of bhavana?"

"The capitol of Cuba?"

"Good, you've made a joke."

"You're not laughing."

"Bhavana is an intense level of meditation that calls into being the subject of the meditation. You've done this unintentionally. Only the most evolved guru, expert in the discarding of the self and the employment of mantra and symbols can do this. In our short time together I see that you're not that."

"So what happened?"

"You prayed to me during your drive."

"You know how your thoughts run wild on a long drive? I was kidding around."

"Other conditions provoked me into revealing myself."

"The rocks in the back of the truck?"

"I apologize, can I get you something to drink."

"Juice, I guess."

While he goes to the kitchen, I study his room, sparse furnishings for a God. I've seen the rug in Target.

"Did your mother warn you about praying to strange Gods?" He hands me room temperature tomato juice.

"I know all about you, Lord Shiva. I've been to India."

"You told me in the car."

"Pleased to meet you but how do I rate this honor?"

"Bhavana requires the consumption of meat, grain, fish and the internalizing of sexual desire."

"I had MacDonald's for lunch."

"Yesterday?"

"It was Thanksgiving. I had beer, clams and lots of turkey."

"Withholding of sexual release?"

"If that's all it takes, I would have met you by now."

"The lingas gave you access to me."

"Great, can I get paid and go? I have a long drive ahead of me."

"I want to ask you a question but before you answer, please remember that I'm a Hindu God. I am without beginning or end and I can see your heart, mind and secret desires. So please don't lie, we have such limited time. Where is the missing case?"

"I don't know."

Casual as a man tipping his hat, Shiva peels his beeti back. His third eye is a camera flash held to the tip of my nose; it blinds me. I'm knocked off my chair.

"Perhaps we will have time for tea." I hear his voice from a long way off.

from the rooftop of the house on the hill

the night is a flashlight beneath an Army blanket

a breeze stirs the curtains into mermaid's hair

on pillows speckled with mirror chips

I lie beside you - allergic to sleep

your hip is an inviting foothill

lips wet with cooking oil

a kiss of tanduri hors d'oeuvre

your husband on business in Delhi

"You wrote this?" Shiva is reading from my collection of poems. I hear pages turning. My eyes are swollen shut from trauma.

"I was in college."

"And now?"

"I don't write poetry anymore. What did you do to my eyes?"

"You sent this collection to an Indian publisher."

"If you know that, you know it never went anywhere."

"We have our own poets."

"That occurred to me."

"And in the States?"

"They are the cornerstone of my unpublished efforts."

"Did your Indian hosts know you were lusting after their wives and daughters?"

"It's all fantasy. I couldn't get to first base in Bihar. What did you do to my eyes?"

"Relax, they will recover. I'm afraid I'm a God with a short temper."

"You didn't buy my story?"

"One reason Gods don't talk to men is that men insult us with everything they say. Even their humblest prayers seem impertinent."

"I apologize; it's difficult to conceive I'm speaking with a Hindu deity."

"The Hindu deity – see what I mean?"

"Sorry, can I have my eyes back?"

"Not yet. It will save us time if you don't try to lie to me. Forget your stories. I am the Destroyer out to destroy lies and theft."

"With four arms and the name Destroyer you could rule Wrestlemania."

"I wonder if you think my time is important to me."

"We're back to the missing case?"

"You feel you must be loyal to your Sikh friend."

"Not anymore, I just wanna get paid and go."

"The missing case, please?"

"Why don't you discuss this directly with Surrinder? I'm just doing what I'm told. He'll be in his office on Monday."

My neck snaps backwards. He's punched light into my blind eyes.

"The tears of death are famine and disease. Anger chains man to the wheel of death and rebirth." I wake in the middle of Shiva's discourse. He is pacing around in his white tablecloth. His four arms are gesturing in a way that would drive an orchestra crazy. Is he rehearsing a sermon or am I meant to be following? I'm laid out on daybed, my eyes stewing in chlorine.

"Are you saying anything I need to hear because I missed the first part?" My eyesight is returning but I'm looking through a neglected aquarium.

"You have a long drive ahead of you. Think on what I have told you."

"Where am I going?"

"To get the fifth case."

"I don't..."

"Please, no more lies, ponder on what I have shared with you. It will provide you stamina."

I get off the bed and walk to the window. Down in the driveway Surrinder's truck sits with an empty cargo bed.

"Are you paying me?"

Shiva hands me bills folded in half. I hold them to the tip of my nose and can tell the outer one is a hundred dollar note. I have the good manners not to count money in front of a God. With the cash in my hand, my confidence begins to bleed back into me. I decide to be sympathetic.

"I really don't have access to that case. I wish I could get you what you think you're owed. If there's been a mistake, I'm sure Surrinder will rectify it. I'll make certain he knows how serious you are." A salesman is always on the side of the person he is speaking to.

"I'm expecting you for tea tomorrow." His hair is Bob Marley homage.

"I really don't see that happening." In sales, never say "No" outright.

"We mustn't waste time."

"What makes you think he's just going to give it to me? It's locked up in his garage. He's not even at home. He's in San Francisco."

"This is for you to consider during your drive."

"Please don't zap me with the magic eye but really this is between you and Surrinder. I'm a Roman Catholic. Jesus Christ is my God. Are you familiar with him?"

"We call him The New Guy."

"Well, he's my master. Can't you get a Hindu to help you?"

"Did I explain about my short temper?" Shiva lies down on the bed I just got off.

"Okay I'll figure something out and I'll call you." Sales is about getting out the door when you still have your feet under you.

"Where are my keys?"

Shiva opens the lower hand on his right side. The keys shine against his dark palm. He closes it as I reach for them.

"Come sit beside me," he pats the daybed.

I plop down crushing my better judgment.

"Closer." His voice is soothing now.

I stand up and sit down a half cheek closer.

"Kiss me." The black dreadlocks thick as hickory roots turn a Harlow yellow. His face morphs into a version of a Jane Mansfield. Breasts rise as his garment recedes. He's cherry-picking ingredients from a teenage wet dream.

"Nice." My lips move to a neck perfumed as bougainvillea. I taste vanilla and cherry soda. My hands cup breasts cool as wine sacs. My linga responds to a fire alarm. Reaching beneath his lungi, I find Shiva half-transformed.

"Gods are both male and female," he says, teasing me.

"Okay, I'll bring up the missing case."

"How kind of you."

With a roll of his hips away and then back, Shiva reveals the Delta of Venus, the scented grotto, the Garden of Eden, the Bermuda triangle. It's the divine furrow of Sita that winks at me, nips my finger like a koi in a pool. I undress as if my clothes are on fire.

Siddhi is the possession of supernatural powers by a mortal. When I spring from Shiva's bed after a profound nap, my mind and eyes are clear. I have a sacred bounce to my step. I throw a five-punch combination at a valet mirror before putting my pants on and going downstairs. Shiva has returned to being a four-armed Thoreau making coffee.

"Milk and two sugars," I say.

"You have no need to tell me."

"If you know everything, why question me?"

"I had to know if you would lie to me."

"I'm a salesman."

"Drink and go and come straight back."

"I suppose I have no choice."

"Choice is an illusion. Men are controlled by Gods as fickle as any mortal. It's your dharma to amuse us."

"There's something else bothering you." In sales, you have to read between the lines.

"We are in Kali Yoga, the shortest cycle in a spiritual age, a period in which the motives of men are most debased."

"You're looking at me when you say that."

"Did you do anything in India besides try to seduce women with awkward poetry?"

"I kissed Mother Theresa."

"Did it do you any good?"

"The day's not over yet your highest Highness. Hey I loved the part where you became Sputa Das Gupta. You really touched every note."

"You didn't exactly internalize."

"Sorry."

Shiva stirs his tea, I'm in a great mood and I don't feel like leaving.

"Did you, you know, enjoy that?" I'm blushing.

"Idiot, man's ingratitude is the number one reason God's get enraged. Is there no end to your stupidity?"

"One question please, why the big deal over the linga?"

"I've watched Swamis, Sahdies, Gurus, Mystics and Masters ride west and plunder the riches of America. The best of them can't carry my katch.

"You haven't been properly promoted."

"I'm hearing this from you?"

"Fair enough but what held you up?"

"Marital problems, I'm wed to an insanely jealous Goddess. I couldn't get away from her for ages."

"Pussy whipped." I drain my coffee. "Where is she?"

"I cursed her to roam the earth. I had to. She was standing in the way of my career."

"Do you know where she is?"

"The dharma of a God is to act as a God and not concern oneself with the actions of others."

"I'm taking that as a no. She must have great powers."

"She has the spark of creation in her yoni. Her nipples drip morphine; her kiss is the kiss of a cobra."

"Sounds like you miss her."

"Get out already with your stupid sales tricks."

"Why me, can't you get the lingas yourself?"

"Of course I can, I can level Bayside with my third eye. If I do, what credit goes to you? How have you redeemed yourself for your stupid lies? What will my followers think of a God who does his own legwork?"

"So I'm doing this to save my soul?"

"I am Shiva the Destroyer. I destroy the stupid, the blind, those who clog the path of salvation."

"I'd better get going." I hear the truck in the driveway start.

"How did you do that?" I'm impressed until I see the key fob has a remote starter I hadn't noticed.

He hands me the keys.

"Go before I burn you to the ground."

When one has Siddhi in their blood, it emanates like curry through the pores. I am so refreshed that driving back to Bayside seems simple as steering south. It's predawn dark. I seem sure of where I'm going while zooming past woods where Thoreau talked to God while sidestepping deer ticks. My ears still ring from the aftershocks of epic lovemaking. My organ is pixilated as a Japanese porn cartoon. I'm already justifying my betrayal to Surrinder. I'm no longer in control of my actions; I'm answering to a higher power.

Henry David Thoreau died of tuberculosis at age 45 - so much for the benefits of camping. In 1846 he lives beside a pond in a shack the size of a Frigidaire carton. Seven years later he publishes Walden Pond. Six years after its release, he dies broke and unnoticed.

In 1978 Jimmy Carter brought a set of Thoreau's journals to the Prime Minister of India who proclaimed Henry D "perhaps even greater than Gandhi."

After a month in India, my college arts team takes recess in Katmandu, Nepal. It's a kingdom full of Santa helpers. Walking down the street, I appear a shot blocker. I see the world as John must see it. I'm looking into second story windows. Our hotel bus takes us to the mountaintop casino.

"Pair a dice lost," Randy quips as we approach a castle-like gambling fortress.

I miss the bus back to the hotel and find myself broke and impaired in a foreign country. I sit on the curb and shiver to clear my head. I'm a scar-faced fighter chewing a stick. Living off my wits, my eyes are quick to spot an easy touch. I'm fighting local champs in backwater ports. I'm Hemingway, Henry Miller, Jack Dempsey and Indiana Jones. Back home I got a girl but tonight I'm a world away with no way to call. Another bus pulls up and I ride back to my four star hotel to wash my socks in the sink.

In the morning I go for a walk and get a haircut. I jump rope in the hotel garden. Dave, my roommate, is felled by an intestinal crisis. I'm staying out of the room as much as possible in case he's contagious. At midday I tiptoe in to make sure he's still breathing. Using my etch-a-sketch I portray his condition; asleep on his side with his head underneath a pillow. I show it to the guys at dinner. We are joined by Mr. Tagore, the Rotary Governor who has come from Bihar to buy us dinner.

"You are the poet I am told." He leans toward me.

I blush at the title. "It's not for me to say." Mr. Tagore seems pleased at my reply.

"Hey Nat King Cole pass the panee," John says and the others laugh.

My return is side B of the ride to Carlisle. What had been on the right is now on the left. I pass the Rotary Club restaurant. At 7:45 A.M. only the parking lot lights are on. I pull over to count the money Shiva gave me. The outside bill is the only one whole. The other four have been cut in half. He's not taking any chances with me. I consider turning back but never touch my turn signal. He got me good. I bet he sensed I wasn't brought up to double check the word of God. In sales you can't be a crybaby. I'm still in the game and I may have a chance to reverse my fortunes.

What went on in Shiva's bed is a house on fire inside me. I feel more alive than ever before. I'm smiling and driving, driving and smiling, changing lanes for no reason. My linga is sleepy as a Serengeti lion after an all you can eat water buffalo buffet. I'm living life, not understanding it.

When I reach Bayside I will be faced with the moment where I betray either Surrinder or Shiva. Right now my money is on me returning to Carlisle and perhaps another afternoon in the arms of a God. I'm a long drive away from making that call. No telling my mood when I get home, the only thing I'm sure of is my promise to Rose.

The dharma of man is to worship God. By hijacking that linga, Surrinder has insulted the Lord of Destruction. I'm in the middle and I'm not being properly compensated. Bayside to Carlisle or Carlisle to Bayside it's no short hop – a tank and a half of gas in either direction.

After-shocks from rolling around on Shiva's daybed rock my boxer shorts. I recall a moment when I struggled with the tight white uniform of a nurse in white stilettos. Her Monroe hair and Valentine red lipstick are drawn from an erotic cartoon. She's a flat-chest witch too hot to wait for me to undress her. It's a summer afternoon and we're alone in a hospital ward. This is just one of the scenes that replay in my head. They keep me focused on returning to Carlisle. I burst out of Rhode Island and into Connecticut, chased by sirens.

As my college road trip exits Mother Theresa's courtyard, we meet a teenage mom holding a baby with a cleft palate. She is waiting for one of the sisters to come and take her child away. My eyes are stinging. As a kid, my friends and I had a fort with more amenities than the Sisters of Mercy orphanage. Mother Theresa has advised us, "Love till it hurts."

164

Feeling like a firefly approaching a klieg light, I bite my tongue over my petty complaints. An eighty year old lady supervises a sinkhole of humanity and I bitch about not getting a hot shower. Sitting in our car, I watch the girl with the giveaway baby. I could snatch the brat and watch her grow up to be an ice skating star or a piano teacher to special needs kids. Sure, red tape is everybody's excuse. As we pull away, I accuse myself of being a weak and selfish boy scared of a baby with an open upper lip.

Supta gallops with flaming hair

her stallion's hooves toss dirt bombs

hoof prints become tide pools

she's chased by her reflection in the river

John is my dead brother

lying beside me

in the bed we share

atop the Dhunbad auto dealership

at the aluminum plant lecture

I picture you in bed

something you said makes me

laugh aloud without explanation

Recalling my poems reminds me of what a jerk I was, a fake in a red blazer sitting beside Dr. Tagore. I promise myself to get my collection out and refresh it; improve everything. I should have done it years ago. HDT commented on "the lonely activity of composition". I was too young to sit down and work at writing. I was walking, talking, and shaking hands, having chosen the sport of sales.

Images of Shiva portray him holding objects in his four hands. The usual lineup is a drum, a flame, a sword, and another eye. With the drum he summons the dawn of creation and with the flame he lays it to waste. His sword is a show piece. The eye is redundant; if anyone doesn't need an extra eye it's this dude.

Because Brahma is the first born son of the cosmos, he enjoys special stature. Vishnu is honored in the Bagadha-Gita. Of the two major Hindu epics, it's the one that's been better promoted. Shiva is stuck with the linga as his icon. The stone is often decorated with garland and beads. At times multiple faces are carved onto the stone suggesting duplicity inspired by the penis.

Dave comes to life on the day we leave Nepal. He missed our flight around Everest and the night at the casino. It took four days in bed before he and his intestines could be friends again.

"I prayed to get better," Dave whispers to me to let me know how bad it had been. Dave's an outspoken cynic of all religions. Back in India we spend the night in the Delhi Airport Retirement room – like sleeping at Mini-Storage.

Thoreau died in 1862, a year after the Civil War kicked off. At forty-five he couldn't be called too old to fight. He was rugged enough to live outdoors and shoot his mouth off about slavery. His tuberculosis would have made him useless but for a guy who loved to bitch about authority, the Army would've been a hoot.

As with other mystics, ascetics, holy men and neighborhood crackpots, people kept their distance from Henry. Rumor was he once kicked the ass of two guys who were hanging around Concord trying to get laid. Out at Walden Pond he got so pissed at a woodchuck for eating his bean plants, he killed the bitch and ate it. He didn't run in any social circles. Gordon quoted Thoreau as saying, "He who seeks friends is not worthy of his own company." No surprise; HDT didn't run for office.

While unzipping I-95, I ask myself to devise a sales strategy. I was fired Tuesday; now it's Saturday and I'm about to break the first rule in sales - don't bite the hand that feeds you. I'm uncertain of the karma I'm creating. I have to return Surrinder's truck unless I intend to steal it along with his prized stone. My car is in his driveway. I could try reaching his wife; she has a home on Long Island. Why would she open the garage and let me take the linga? It was her idea to hold it back. She rarely says more than two words to me and I've been dealing with Surrinder for years. I give her that prayer hands greeting and throw an "Accha" around to remind her I'm a devoted fan of her homeland. I don't even know her proper first name. Surrinder calls her Mom but I'm not sure she has children.

If I did get her on the phone, I'd be faced with convincing a frugal Hindu housewife to part with a valued stone while her husband is out of town. That's a tall order for me and I can make cow pie taste like Godiva. Better for me to just pop the garage door, muscle the stone into my car and head back to Carlisle. The artist is a man of action I remind myself. On the long drive back, I'll have time to consider what to say to Surrinder before he cuts my throat.

One time an Evergreen Airline sales rep closed the door of her motel room with her naked leg being the last thing to disappear behind it. She had been sunbathing at the pool and had to know I was studying her. Her room was a few steps away from her lounge chair. It was early enough that most guests were still in their rooms. I had seen her at a sales party the night before, drinking, laughing and throwing her head back. Somehow, Shiva brought that girl back to me years after I froze at saying hello to her. Two hours from home I'm dreaming awake with a purring housecat in my lap.

219th Street, just south of Horace Harding Boulevard is a block of attached homes with driveways where lawns should be. Surrinder's place is easy to miss even if you've been there before. It's a three story home in a line of three story homes, tight as beads on a rosary. Garage door, storm door, garage door, storm door, from one end of the block to the other - how do people live like this? College kids and newlyweds gravitate here. Surrinder sticks out like the magician at a kid's party.

It's 7 pm on Saturday evening. I got home earlier this afternoon but couldn't get much sleep. Now I'm approaching the peeling paint on Surrinder's garage door under cover of darkness. I'm armed with a souvenir pocket knife with side plates of the Taj. Before doing anything criminal, I give the handle a sharp jerk in hope it opens. Of course it's locked. It's okay to be optimistic but avoid pipe dreams. I set about 'jimmying' the lock, something I've seen done on TV and nowhere else. Resolved to running a chain from my front bumper to the garage door, I expect I'll pull the door off its track enough to sneak inside. Better get extra money in Carlisle or I'll wind up eating the repair. Before I can get one step into my crackpot game plan, I see Surrinder's wife standing at the door. I drop the switchblade and fold my hands.

"Sorry Mom, I didn't want to bother you." She beckons me inside. At her kitchen table she sets a glass of juice on a saucer in front of me

. "I know your husband is away but I really have to get that last linga. You see the people in Carlisle know you're holding it back and

169

they're hurt. I didn't get paid what I was owed and I had to promise I would bring it back or I will have an angry God after my ass."

I'm talking too fast, I sound scattered. I suspect she hasn't followed a word of what I've said. She indicates I should drink the juice. I'm breaking into her house but she's worried I'm thirsty. In a million billion years I will never understand the Indian woman.

"To you, Mom," I take a gulp that would make any Mother proud. She smiles and I put up my hand up to say no more. The juice should have been refrigerated.

"I'll explain everything when I get back but I've got to grab that baby and go. Rest assured I'm making sure Surrinder gets the best deal possible. I'm looking for a nice reward for all of us from what I'm doing."

I have no idea if she's listening. I must have a look on my face because she's smiling. Words are coming out of my mouth like an intermission crowd spilling into a theater lobby.

There's a radio playing Hindi rock. I can pick out the dulcimer and the sitar. Rooming with John made me an expert on Indian musical instruments. That guy could play the Syncopated Clock on a coffee can.

I'm lying in bed watching Surrinder's wife dance a dance of seduction. Her nightdress catches light off the ceiling lamp. The gown parts and I see parts too fine to belong to Surrinder's Mom. I finally get that I've been slipped a Hindu Mickey.

I jump out of bed and start throwing my clothes off. She goes into another room and returns with the linga in her arms. I can't believe she's carrying it. She sets it on the foot of the bed. After dimming the overhead, she sweeps around the room lighting candles like a convent Mother.

Beside me in bed, I take her with the poise and confidence of a salesman. Sales guys are often indulgent sexually. With daily access to the outside world, they are bombarded by temptations. The urge to reward themselves for doing the job no one else wants to do leads to them taking liberties on company time. No respect is accorded their position. They are described as a necessary evil.

With my feet pressing the linga against the foot board, I ripple like a caterpillar. My love maiden rides me, a flame on my wick. Reflections wink off her nose ring; the beeti on her forehead sways as a lighted buoy.

In the space of the last twenty four hours, I've twice had sexual intercourse in the presence of a linga. I need to get one of these stones. Up in Carlisle, I loved the way Shiva became different women in my life but down here in Bayside it's another kind of baseball. I'm boss here. With Surrinder out of town, I sense his wife looking at me in an all new half light. After an hour in bed, she's calm enough to cuddle with. I have made her my prisoner for the evening. I am Rama stretching the sacred bow. I inscribe with a magic saber, Sanskrit across her tummy.

I wake alone in bed. Getting up too fast, I have to lie right back down. Mrs. Surrinder is sitting at the kitchen table shelling peas. I kiss her on the top of the head and then kneel beside her chair and force my head into her lap. She's back to being a middle age woman with bulging arms and midsection. Her eyes are no longer lined and her jewelry's muted. She touches her lips to the back of my hand to indicate submission. I go outside to take my car out of the driveway and put Surrinder's in. I open my car door and see the giant linga strapped into my passenger seat like a preschooler. She is at the driver side window.

"Say your name," I ask.

"Shasta."

"Of course," I act like I knew but forgot.

"I'm going to protect you and your husband by getting what's due you." I've fallen back into that rattling sales screech.

"Protect yourself. It is not permitted for a mortal to be in the company of a God." She touches my hand.

"Why do you say that? Did I talk in my sleep?"

"By the way you made love; I knew you had been in proximity with the Divine."

"You weren't bad either."

I start toward home. I've got the rock and I'm already late so why rush? My car turns with a mind of its own. I approach the Whitestone

172

Bridge with no power to change direction. I should be getting a night's sleep at home. As a parting gesture, Shasta put her husband's EZ pass on my windshield.

The return to Carlisle is a book I'm rereading. Some plot points were missed on the first two trips; other scenes have the impact of a character's death. Certain billboards pulse a memory lamp. I recall exactly what I was thinking when I passed these spots yesterday. That seems a long time ago. I was a different guy then, naïve and so un-otherworldly. I count up the women I've had sex with and then add two. If I knew then what I know now, each of them would be missing me. I'm up to my ears with lovemaking techniques from the Kama Sutra. My windshield's been washed.

My best hope is to get out of Carlisle with the money due me and something extra for Surrinder. I'll explain it all as a win/win. Shiva doesn't care about money; Surrinder should have never held the rock back. He succumbed to seller's remorse. I drop my seatback to the two o'clock position. I'm not going to speed or change lanes. I'm driving my own car now.

Turn in your hand like a smooth stone any victory you may recall. Steel yourself for an upcoming ordeal by rooting around in that top drawer of grade school track medals. Confidence is born of demonstrated ability. I've got in and out jams in the past. This is the same only bigger.

When I take my eyes off my thoughts, they fly back to Surrinder's wife. The bath I had inside her, how I swayed in her hammock, drank her warm beer. She is the India I fell in love with but never kissed. My pores enlarge, my blood swirls through my veins like a super-collider. I snap my steering wheel to the right. Wet dreaming has me changing lanes without signaling. I know the woman I had sex with was not Surrinder's wife. If she was, he would never leave home.

Pushing north on I-95. I try to guess what Thoreau would do if he were in my shoes. Losing $400 would not sit well with that cheapskate. On the other hand, he wouldn't risk his future for pocket money. Loyalty was important to HDT. Since Surrinder is not here to advise me, my devotion to him decreases with every mile marker. The sex trance whipped on me by Lord Shiva has been neutralized by Shasta. I'm caught between a rock and hardened place. I am a slave to earthly pleasure. I imagine Henry shaking his bearded head over my devotion to yoni. Reaching over to stroke the crown of the linga relaxes me. I announce myself an easy conquest.

Pressing my head against the headrest helps me control my thoughts. They are changing course like a school of fish. I focus on safe driving by imagining pop-up obstacles and exotic wildlife crossings. I'm encouraged that I've started out with a full tank of gas. Stay Awake, Stay Alive - I pass a lighted billboard. It seems simple enough. I don't read the last five pages of a mystery to spare myself the suspense. India taught

174

me not to look beyond today and tomorrow. Watch your gauges and remain in lane. I chant to myself, "You promised; you promised."

above the Buddhist temple in Nepal

sun pours through a trapdoor in the clouds

spotlights cuckoo clock houses

windows underlined by flower boxes

monks in orange robes

feed the shrine monkeys

all is peace at this place

its name means Doorstep of Heaven

at this sacred resting spot

the vagabond son of Man

prayed for safe passage

on his walking tour of India

wandering holy men

kick their flip flops off this cliff

lay down on the holy earth

to die in hope of rising no more

"I know of no more encouraging fact than this. Every man has the ability to elevate himself by conscious endeavor." This is Gordon quoting Thoreau out of my memory bank. I've been elevating and getting elevated these past two days. Whole chunks of memory are surfacing like toys from a flooded basement. The scent of India is all around me; I can hear her tinkling bells. I experience a moment in which my car swells to the size of a fifty story building. I'm looking out into the sky like a fighter pilot. My steering wheel arcs like the Dragon Coaster. My dashboard glows like downtown from a window seat. The linga in the passenger seat is the Goodyear blimp wearing a seatbelt. Clouds wash my car by hand. Just for second, I swell to touch all sides of the world. With a flutter, I shrink down into traffic so fast I feel car sick. I wipe the sweat from my palms on my pants.

Slim chance you fall asleep driving a motorcycle. In a car you're more likely to close your eyes. I've snapped awake from the nudge of rumble strips more than once tonight. It's eleven P.M. on Saturday night of Thanksgiving weekend. The Sandman is kicking sand in my eyes. The rush of Shasta's lovemaking has worn off. I'm wearing ankle weights on my eyelids. There's a sandbag on top of my head testing the will of my neck. You know how you wake up when the book you're reading hits to the floor. I roll my window down and slap myself in the face. I think about my lonely bed, the one I'm driving away from. I imagine myself in a Laz-E-Boy, a cotton futon, a Dux bed, a Sleepy's warehouse. It's no joke; I've got to pull over. I stick my head out the window and wash my face with wind. I take my shoes and socks off and drive barefoot. My blood is thin as chicken bouillon. Hallucinations dance on the road in front of me. Daffy Duck in a hard hat waves a checkered flag. Men in evening wear waltz women in white gowns. A carousel of zebras, the Rockettes appear and disappear. On my right the dark woods roll past me like black clouds. The shoulder is thin as a G-string. Cars pass, some blow their horns. I steer toward a rainbow in the sky. It's the golden arches of McDonalds. I pull into the lot and drop my seat back as far as it will go. It rests on the junk I took from my office the other day. I'm asleep, without turning my headlights off.

When I sit up, I smack my head against a sun visor left in the down position. Its 1:10 A.M. I've been asleep for less than three hours. I shut off my lights in a panic. The car cranks feebly and doesn't catch. I pull my seat up, pump the gas and take three deep breaths. The car comes to life on the second try. A fog rings my brain and colonizes McDonald's. Joining a line of cars exiting the lot, I'm spooked by a square-shaped blind spot. It's on my passenger window. The cars in front of me are not moving so I jump out. YOU ARE PARKED IN A SPOT RESERVED FOR THE HANDICAPPED.

Guilty of course, it's one of those stickers that require a tub of hot water and a razor blade to remove. I flash on the idea that I've locked

177

myself out of the car so I jump back in. I can't understand the time it's taking to leave when I see I've pulled into the 24 hour drive-up window. Good, I'll have pancakes. When I reach the talking menu board I order. "Sir we don't serve breakfast until 6am."

"Two cheeseburgers and a large coffee, please."

Northbound on I-95, I rip a mouse hole in the coffee lid and sip that pulse of hope that comes with Mickey's brew. I eat a cheeseburger and toss the wrapper on the passenger seat where it rolls to a stop on the spot where my linga should be sitting. I make a U-turn so quick the cheeseburger jumps up my throat. Oncoming cars flash their lights and move aside. They think I don't know I'm driving south in a northbound lane. I pray my speedy backtrack attracts no cop. My coffee has spilled in my lap. As I enter the exit lane of the parking lot, I realize I've never turned my headlights back on. I've been speeding south in a northbound lane with no headlights. I'm sure I've lived longer than I deserve.

I pull into the same space where I was parked. I'm expecting to see the linga sitting there like the kid who the school bus forgot. I get out of the car and do what I always do when I'm in an absolute panic. Sinking my hands deep into the hair on the sides of my head, I begin pacing in an eight step pattern, four up, four back.

"Oh crap, oh crap, oh crap." Never vary script or intonation. Ajada-mantra is an involuntary repetition of a mantra. Your mantra is the uniqueness of your spirit expressed in sound. Knowing your mantra is part of the recipe for approaching transcendentalism.

178

I can recall poems I wrote twenty years ago but have no clue to how a stone sitting in my lap got away from me. Did I forget to lock the door before I fell asleep? Was I so out of it that someone could pull a hundred and twenty pound stone out of my car without me waking? Has Shiva put devotees on my tail? Am I being punished for being familiar with divinities? I get on my knees and press my head on the rear bumper of my car. A rounded bolt head creates a circle in the center of my forehead. I pray to Jesus, asking him to take an immediate interest in my predicament. I don't care if anyone sees me. I'm not afraid to ask the Lord's protection.

When my knees hurt, I get up. I circle the edge of the rest stop looking in trash barrels and the dumpster behind Mickey D's. I walk against the line of cars inching toward the drive-up window. Many are carpools headed toward colleges - perhaps a frat house got my baby. I look under tractor trailers and idling tour buses. I step into the brush and peer down trails. Returning to my car, I find a second sticker that matches the first stuck on my driver side window. I get in the car. It's November and I'm wearing a light jacket. I resolve to sit in the car until an acceptable plan emerges. As a salesman, I thrive in crisis.

"The amount of happiness in your life is dictated by the quality of your thoughts," Marcus Aurellias said this. I'm reviewing the Hindu folktale Ramayana inside my head because it's an epic tale of tribulation and gives me something to do while waiting to kill the person who put the stickers on my windows.

This is the version of Ramayana told on my college tour. We were in the garden at a retirement house in Barbil. The teller's name is Babu. He brags he has never worked a day in his life.

"So you're clergy." I see Frank elbow Randy.

Babu includes names and descriptions of lesser characters; he doesn't have to get up in the morning. Ramayana is an epic tale; episodes are included at the whim of the teller. I'm only giving you the good parts.

Rama, the self-exiled son and his wife Sita live with his brother Lakshmania. A girl demon, Rakshasi approaches Rama while he is out hunting. She has the power to take the form of anyone you desire. She tries to seduce Rama by pretending to be his wife. Rama is not fooled. He becomes the first man to be faithful to his wife while on a hunting trip.

Rama invites Rakshasi back to his camp so she can be catnip for his brother who has gone into exile stag. It stands to reason that his brother would jump out of his upturned sandals over a girl who could be any woman you wanted her to be. Instead of taking advantage of his brother's thoughtfulness, Lakshmania cuts off the she-demons nose and ears. She runs crying to her dad. Her father and brother go to war with Rama over the next six reels of wide screen Technicolor.

Why would a guy who is shacked up with his brother and his hot sister-in-law turn down yoni from a demon queen? Sita pads around in her under things, her brother-in-law is not blind. She's across the hall hitting high notes with his brother while he's alone with his linga. Why turn away a woman wishing to be possessed by a man? Later in the story Rama's wife, Sita is kidnapped. She drops jewelry to mark her trail. Rama finds a piece but isn't sure if it's hers. Lakshmania assures him it belongs to his wife.

"You know my wife's toe ring?"

The tale of Ramayana teaches us that dharma is the code of righteous living. No man should shirk the obligation to be himself. Rama exiles himself because he is a warrior by nature. He cannot change his role in life and I can't change mine. The folly of my sales career is underlined by this wicked loop from Bayside to Carlisle.

The Hindu epic insists that every man confront the wrongs that surround him. An eventual union with God will only come through personal efforts. It is said that anyone who reads the Ramayana is free from sin. This is brilliant marketing by Shiva who conceived the story and had it ghosted by Valmiki.

I'm first on line when they start serving breakfast at McDonalds. I order a Sausage McMuffin with egg and a large coffee. I'm moving mummy-like around the tables. Sleeping across bucket seats has crippled me. Without the linga, I don't know whether to go forward or back. I won't have the situational awareness to consider my options until I drink this coffee. Nothing is settled until the sun comes up. The morning shift employees are loud and making jokes. They seem to know I've been sleeping in my car. The homeless are key consumers at the golden arches.

After breakfast I use a cup of hot water from McDonalds and a single-edge razor from a box of office supplies on the back seat of my car and start scraping the stickers off. It's Sunday morning on Thanksgiving weekend. I'm cold, my hands are cramped and I have no holder for the blade. After forty minutes, I quit without being finished. My fingers are protesting and blowing on them doesn't help.

I go to the restroom in McDonald's. Their coffee has unbound me. I wash my face and hands and brush my teeth with my finger tip. I must have slept with my head pressed against my watch face because there's a circle in the center of my forehead that surrounds the one lifted off my bumper. It inspires me to a reopen my investigation.

At the far end of the parking lot, I descend a deer trail I only looked down last night. With the sun coming up, I sidestep downhill until I hear water. Through evergreens, I see a stream like a sparkling necktie. It's hardly deep enough to cover a snow tire that sits midstream like a Cheerio.

I stop when I smell a bidi. The aroma of those Indian fags is imbedded in my memory bank. Part of the charm and serenity of the Indian people can be credited to their being whacked on bidi, betel nut, and pan. America's character is tied to tobacco. We were a tougher country when everybody smoked and wore hats. Guys won a big war, had four kids and drove a Chevrolet. Today grown men skateboard, you can't leave your car unlocked and the handicapped are assigned the best parking spaces.

I squat in an ambush pose. Voices come up from the creek. A garbage truck lifting the dumpster in the parking lot provides me the cover I need to creep closer. An Indian couple squats on a strip of shore below me. He's stirring the water with a stick. She's old enough to be his mother. They are Hindu Indians wearing white pajamas and sandals. They're both smoking.

"Good morning." I speak too loud and startle them. They huddle close as if in danger. "Namaste," I put my hands in prayer shape. "I was out stretching my legs and I caught a whiff of your bidi. Could I trouble you for one?"

They are staring at me and the circles on my forehead.

"You guys doing a little early morning fishing?" I make a hand motion suggesting a fish swimming; my Kara bracelet catches the sun. There are no poles or lines in sight.

"I'm headed north to Carlisle, cute little place. Say have you guys ever been to Patna?" It is the nature of a salesman to fill a void.

The young man steps away from his mother and says something in Hindi that I don't understand. He's shrill as a rear-ended cabbie. His mother pulls him back and speaks sharply, nodding toward the center of my forehead. She smiles and puts her hands together. She turns to her son and he pulls a bidi from his sleeve and lights it for me. I stand and smoke while they sidestep uphill. He goes first and pulls his Mother's behind him; their hands are joined like a wedding couple.

Once they're gone I start scouting around for clues about what they were doing down here. Footprints along the bank lead me upstream to a small falls. The bank arcs until it rises six feet above the stream. In an eddy pool, my linga sits like a fat man in a half-full bath. I don't know how I'm going to rescue it but I'm going to.

Salesmen work alone. They can't run back to the office every time they meet an obstacle. Limited authority is not an excuse. They need to pull the trigger to close a deal.

From the trunk of my car, I get out a luggage caddy, a reel of clothesline, and an oven mitt. I find a pair of totes given to me on Father's Day and never worn. I pull them on and cross the parking lot like a flight attendant wearing an oven mitt.

Carrying the luggage caddy and the line, I move upstream deliberate as a mine-sweeper. The water is deep enough to cover the insteps of my Totes. The banks of the creek rise as the creek bed deepens. Water slips down the backs of my boots and soaks my sneakers. The sun is no consolation on this November morning – I'm freezing my ass off. I can't help projecting Thoreau against the foliage that surrounds me. I can identify cypress ferns, blackberries and alfadale. To Thoreau, this is a trip to Whole Foods.

It's the kind of morning you want to catch a touchdown pass - a day when you look so cool in your hipster scarf and suede jacket. A wonderful sunny Sunday after Thanksgiving, I'm spending in ice water. Strolling down the center of a stream that doodles on Eastern Connecticut, I'm a cranky naturalist. The water is ankle-high as I approach my stone sitting like Humpty Dumpty in the kiddie pool. I'm sure the mom and son have everything to do with the rock winding up here but I have no time to waste wondering why. Thoreau said, "We do not choose our themes but are chosen by them." While pulling the stone onto the opened luggage caddy, my hands slip and I sit backwards in the stream. I'm soaked through to my shorts. I have cold water in my wallet.

"Our only obligation is to rise to a new and more perfect day," (Gordon quoting HDT). I curse aloud in words I'd never use in front of my mother. Then I get up and go; in sales don't lose focus. There's a difference between a jam, a jelly, and a preserve but in every case you don't want them on the seat of your pants.

I crisscross the nylon straps of the luggage caddy so they hold the stone upright like a fat guy wearing a bandolier. I put the nylon line around the handle of the luggage caddy and start dragging my treasure home like caveman seducing a cave girl who has five foot long pony tail. The oven mitt keeps the line from cutting into my hand. The wheels of the luggage caddy don't turn but I yank them over rocks and across pebble beds. Walking backwards I pull like a man making a hammer throw. Turning forward with the line across my shoulder I trudge downstream.

185

I congratulate myself on my progress when I'm not even half way back. There is still the question of getting the stone up the hill to parking lot – in sales there is little time for idle thought. Thoreau elevated idle thinking to an art form. He was a naturalist who in 1844 fell into a deep meditation during which his campfire slipped its bounds and burned down 300 acres of prime Concord woods.

During the drudgery of pulling a stone along a streambed, my mind ping pongs between Thoreau and Gordon and back.

"The poet is bound to write his own biography." Gordon once counseled me with this Thoreauism when I despaired of ever being noticed. He suggested that I hadn't fully committed myself to writing poetry.

"I don't want to starve to death."

"The poet is the toughest son of the earth." Gordon is channeling Henry. "His is the loftiest written wisdom." He didn't care if I was a good poet or not.

"You're a poet so be a poet, don't cry about the wages -work part time, live simply."

I'm within sight of the point where I entered the water and have the line wrapped around my waist. I plod like a slave hauling cornerstone to a pyramid. I'm soaking wet from the waist down and the day is no less chilly. I have a desperate need to pee although I'm dehydrated. Having fallen three times, all I need is a crown of thorns and a face cloth. I've

186

cursed Surrinder and Shiva and prayed for the Lord's mercy. During my snail crawl, I took a swing at saying the Rosary.

Beached at my destination, the linga suggests a sea turtle in deep siesta. The hillside I have to ascend is a sandy Lombard Street. I return to the car with the half-scraped-off stickers on the windows. I back the car into the parking spot closest to the trail leading to the stream. I tie the line to the back bumper of my car. Unspooled, it stretches halfway to where I need it to be. The linga lies in the grip of a luggage cart. Sitting on my wet ass, I dig my heels into the earth and jerk the luggage caddy upward in a thousand small steps. When I reach my line, I tie it to the handle of the caddy and kiss my stone on the crown of its head. Up in the car I pull forward and picture the linga ascending through underbrush. After a trio of false starts, the wheels of the luggage cart come alive on the pavement of the parking lot. The line blocks a stretch of parking spaces and cars are sounding their horns. I get out, drop the line off my bumper and roll my rescued rock into the main dining room at McDonald's. I'm freezing cold and my legs are thumping like jungle drums. I treat myself to pancakes.

You can't dry something off while wearing it. I give up on a slow dance with the blower in Mickey D's men's room. I'm going to have to find a Laundromat. As I roll the stone back toward my car, it starts snowing.

Off 95 in Groton a Laundromat is filled with crew cuts watching an NFL pre-game show. I strip down and throw everything below the waist including my sneakers into a dryer. Using a beach towel I carry in my trunk, I cover up enough to avoid scandal. The cadets snicker and I hear laughing. I'm aware that I'm wearing a Jets sweatshirt in New England. It's warm enough with the dryers all going but every time someone opens the door I get an ice pop up my ass. I can hear my wallet thumping along with my sneakers. I'm sitting on a bench wrapped in a towel and holding cash in my hand. I must look like Gandhi changing currency.

In the window of the dryer, my shirt wrestles my jeans. I'm in no hurry to go because the snow is falling harder. As water boy, I ride the bench. I have $37 left to my name. The hundred dollar bills cut in half are in my wallet. With my bare feet on an overturned wash tub, I set my chin on my knees and hug my lower legs to shake the chills. I close my eyes and recall my time with Shasta.

You don't talk to her, you touch her. It's a date with a cat. Her eyes flash green in the dark. Her breath is sweet air. I'm a surfboard riding her curl, at one with the Indian Ocean.

My eyes open from the quiet of the dryer being off. The football fans are gone and the TV is black. An old woman at a table folds clothes using a wood block to shoo wrinkles. I'm aware of a righteous erection. Outside the storefront, snow falls straight as parachuted supplies. It would be a folly to start driving. Careful to turn my erection toward the wall, I stand and stretch till I'm on my toes. Buzzing with ideas about what to do next, I open the dryer; my laundry is gone.

I stare out the window wondering if my clothes might have gone back to the car on their own - in a kind of wardrobe mutiny. Scavenging

188

the garbage can and lost item bin, I find a pair of shorts that I keep closed with a safety pin. I run back to my car barefoot, drying my feet with the bath towel once inside. Thank God I left my Totes in the car. I put them on. My linga lies on the floor like a hostage. The keys are under the seat where I left them so I start the car. I'm an Eskimo revving up his igloo. Peering through the geisha fans drawn by my windshield wipers, I put the car in gear.

I expect the Patriot fans are the clothes kidnappers hiding out at the nearest sports bar. They may be debating over when to give me back my wash. There is always one sensible individual who doesn't see the humor in this type of stunt. I'm counting on recognizing him. I double park outside a bar on the end of the street. I'll walk in with Totes, checkered shorts, JETS sweatshirt and bath towel. Everyone will applaud; I'll be treated to beer.

Out of the car, I cup my hand against the front window and see two old men sitting at the bar. Three TV's are trained on them. All are showing the same football game.

I go back to my car and start driving. A salesman is bombarded with events designed to put him off course. There are a thousand reasons for staying put; snow is only the most popular. I can't let weather, clothes or a sense of foreboding get in my way. I intend to complete my appointed rounds. I don't have my wallet or driver's license and the heater in the car is weak. Amazing what you think you need to travel yet you travel well without. I slap my hands together "Now you're talking like Thoreau."

189

I'm not obliged to eliminate injustice, only to labor against it. Wow, now I'm even thinking things like he thinks. Henry D has got inside my head, two Indian Goddesses have me by the balls, my feet are freezing and I'm ass sore from driving. There is no part of me that I own outright.

Within sight of the arches, I pull onto the shoulder and rummage in my trunk. I find a green beret from a Halloween parade. Newly outfitted, I'm back in the car. The snowfall has yet to take a breather. If I don't start moving I'll freeze to death. I haven't shaved or brushed my teeth in a long time. An un-barbered holy man, I'm engaged in the transport of a holy stone.

Passing through Concord on a Sunday night, I'm sure of nothing. The radio calls the storm a Nor'easter and no one should be out on the road. The street signs are covered with snow so I'm winging lefts and rights while praying for an oasis. The houses that I pass look like Christmas cards. Pretending that I recognize something, I turn down a road that narrows to a hairpin. I miss the turn and ski down a beginner's hill while standing on the brakes. My quarter panel kisses up to a tree trunk and my headlights spill downhill. They illuminate a small lean-to. I get out of the car and fall on my ass. Pulling myself up, I look around. I'm alone in the silence of a snow forest.

Somewhere at home, I have a merit badge that certifies that I'm not so stupid that I can't build a fire. Using office files and sales reports from the back seat of my car, I turn my career into kindling. The lean-to has an established fire pit in front of it. There is plenty of available wood under a light blanket of white. In a half hour I have a bonfire that makes the lean-to warm as a family room. I get so hot I take my beret off. With a beach chair from my trunk, I set myself close enough to the fire to keep me from freezing. Among my documents I find a copy of THE MOON AND NEVER DYING. It's my collection of poems about India. I read a few and feed a few to the fire. My poetry becomes a fuel to rescue me from a night outdoors. Greater works have served lesser purposes. I'm certain that no one in the world is out looking for me.

on a rocky peak

of twisted trees

men pass in silence

their long robes sweep

the rocks and grass

I glimpse the man-Jesus

in a parish of eagles

his smile, his eyes

a mountain breeze

lifts my hair like wings

Between catnaps, I collect firewood. It takes me twenty minutes to get comfortable after each roundup. A breeze carries away the campfire smoke. I finally get some big wood burning. I can make it to morning; as if I had some other choice. "Nature is outdoors" Henry said. If he was here, I would throw him on the fire.

At dawn my fire remains at my side, faithful as a collie. It breathes hot breath on me - reduced to an ember bed the size of an on-deck circle. I drag my lawn chair close enough to melt my Totes. With my feet up and knees tucked under my chin, I sweat like a human sacrifice.

When I got home from India I took a shot at reading WALDEN. Not the week I got home but a few years later when I was missing Gordon and the guys. I didn't finish it. I remember reading a line from it to my brothers, "We talk of rude and simple times, when men sat about large fires in cold bracing weather with clear heads."That sums up my predicament on the Monday morning after Thanksgiving. My head is painfully clear.

The day gets up on schedule. Birds start chirping, a chipmunk dashes for his train, a fat woodchuck on a tree stump is enthroned as a news dealer. I am amid unheated nature. I love my campfire.

"God culminates in the present." Thoreau. With a floor mat from the car across my lap, I sit like FDR wearing a green beret. I have a stick in my mouth because that's how you brush your teeth in India. I now reside in the kitchen of Transcendentalism.

I return to my car to look for any resource I may have overlooked in the dark. Trying to recall a more preposterous circumstance, I elect to await rescue. It seems to be my only option. If I climb up to the road I slid off, I'll lose my fire. I have yet to hear a plow.

Thoreau said, "What a man thinks of himself determines his fate." My fate is tied to the intelligent design that makes fire a savior for anyone who can start one. Shiva holds a flame in one of his four hands. I hear a snowmobile approaching.

"What in hell are you doing, son?" The sheriff is a giant in snow pants and shaded goggles.

"I took a brodie down that hillside in the middle of the storm." I point uphill as if he might not have noticed my car among the trees.

"That's why we say 'Stay off the roads'. You need to turn out that fire. You're in a restricted area."

"Well, under the circumstances."

"Don't give me circumstances, get it out."

"Yes sir." I flatten my lawn chair and put it back in the car along with the floor mats. Using a cardboard box, I shovel up enough snow to snuff the fire. I police the area and we're ready to go.

"Is that yours?" He's looking at the folder with my poems.

"Yes sir."

"Are those the only clothes you have?"

"Yes sir."

It's warm the way it gets after a heavy snowfall. The sheriff lets me wear his parka. It is way too big and I feel like a papoose on the back of snowmobile. The snow blowing up turns my bare legs raw. I press my face into his back. Once on a straightway, he opens up. He's enjoying my fear. Whiteness zips underneath us until we pull up behind the restaurant where I bought Steve/Lord Shiva a beer the other day – the home of the Carlisle Rotary Club.

I put three dollars on the bar. The sheriff flips open his summons book.

"Coffee please," I ask. The woman behind the bar ignores me.

"He's with you, Sheriff?" she asks. I imagine I must look a sight.

The smell of food from the kitchen has me falling off my barstool.

"I'm issuing this young man a ticket for building a fire on a State Historical sight. He was camping at the Thoreau Memorial."

"That was Walden Pond where you found me?"

"I pull a hundred hippies out of there every year. All of them farting around down there when the posted signs are clear – No fires, No camping."

"To be fair, all the signs were covered by snow. I wasn't camping; my car crashed into the woods."

"That's your story?" The barmaid sets a beer in front of the Sheriff. The dining room is filling up with a lunch meeting.

"It's not a story, it's the truth."

"Why not stay in your car with the heater on."

"I would have run out of gas and my heater is broke."

"You seem to have an answer for everything."

"I haven't an answer for how to get a coffee around here!" My voice is shrill enough to send the barmaid into the kitchen.

"You might take this chance to wash up." The sheriff nods at the door marked GENTS.

In the bathroom mirror, my face is gray from smoke and ash. I have those red circles on my forehead. Three days of beard makes me look homeless. I wash and then wipe my hands dry on my shorts. The place is out of paper towel.

"It's $250 for a first offense. I'll have to hold your license until the fine is paid. If you get caught again, you could do a year in jail."

"I don't have my driver's license."

"You're driving without a license?"

"It was stolen in a Laundromat in Groton."

"Of course." The Sheriff flips his ticket book back open. "You have no other ID?"

"I have an associate here in Carlisle. He will be able to vouch for me and I'll get the money for the fine."

"Call him."

"I can't but if you let me drive over there, I can get this all straightened out."

"Son, your car is property of the Park Police until you can prove ownership, pay the towing fee and pay the damages you did to that hillside."

"No disrespect sir, but you're coming down very hard on a guy who's had a helluva Thanksgiving weekend. I can't pay a cent until I get in touch with my guy."

"Who is he?"

"He runs the Hindu Temple here in town."

"Jesus H. Christ, is it really only Monday?"

He orders me a bowl of bean soup and more coffee. He's off to the pay phone to tell his wife he won't be home for lunch. I alternate sips of soup and coffee.

A man comes out of the dining room and up to the bar. He orders a shot of scotch and knocks it back. He takes a quick look at me and then back to the barmaid.

"Got my balls in a knot, Joanie; the speaker is delayed by the storm. How do I entertain these guys, bird calls?"

"I could recite my poems."

"What did you say?"

"Recite poems I wrote about the Rotary's work in India." I hold up the folder. "Written while I served as Rotary ambassador; this is a Rotary lunch, isn't it?"

"Dave Craddock, President." He hands me his card. I'm ashamed to be without one. We shake hands. I assure him I'm a prize-winning poet and a friend of the Rotary. He goes to a closet and returns with a red sports jacket.

"Please don't bury me." I turn my back as he holds the jacket like a tailor. I shake my arms into the sleeves and do a model's turn. I haven't worn a red blazer in twenty years.

The Sheriff returns from the phone.

"What's going on?" He's looking at Dave Craddock.

"This young man is going to stall the crowd until the speaker arrives."

Dave and the Sheriff drift out of earshot as I conduct a soup and coffee tango. When they return the sheriff explains how "community service" often offsets harsher penalties. Dave promises to wring my neck if I screw up.

"After dinner, I read the news and then I bring you on. Keep going until I tell you to stop."

"I'm a professional," I begin reviewing certain poems. I have no time to edit. I'll read them pretty much the way I wrote them. I'll rehearse in the head. The menu has me unbound.

In the restroom stall, I identify enough material to kill twenty minutes. I'm doing the after-lunch speech I made or heard made at every town we hit in India. Many times the venue had no western toilet. Here in Carlisle I'm enthroned inside a voting booth casting an epic ballot. The bean soup has settled a work stoppage. I've been suffering from a constipation brought on by an absence of facilities. Now I reference a line from the Old Testament – make my enemies into footstools.

I stand in awe of my creation. Imagine two tour buses fighting over one toll booth. If they were alive you could catch them in a trap. I flush and the toilet water rises to the rim like a poured martini. The massive clings to the downhill slope of the bowl like a face on Rushmore. I don't see anything to assist me. Now I can't find toilet paper. I'm going to need help. A rap on the door announces, "He's introducing you." Pulling my pants up, I'm thinking. "It's India!"

"The highest art is to affect the quality of the day." I start my talk with a touch of Thoreau. I just got busted for crashing at his place so why not steal his line as well? In sales you stick with what works, don't experiment. I'm using Gordon's formula because I've watched him wow hundreds of towel heads with this very same sermon.

After a touching retelling of my Rotary sponsored India tour, I feel warmed up enough to try a poem. I'd have more choices about what to read if I hadn't had to leave pages in the loo. My delivery is middle of the road at best and for one or two seconds I'm dead air.

"Aren't they supposed to rhyme?" An old man in the first row turns to the room. Since he isn't asking me, I continue.

"Where's the stuff about Rotary?" The world's worst whisper sails past me. In the event of a mishap during a presentation, keep going. As when crossing a muddy riverbed, do not stop.

I cringe when I see an old man with a cane head toward Gents. I'm walking the floor of the Taj in a poem called "The Bride" when he screams. I act like I didn't hear it. His cane hits the floor; we hear him cry "Medic".

I guess the old goat is a WW1 vet recalling mustard gas. I left that stall humming with the funk of road kill on a hot afternoon. Isn't it basic hospitality to supply your guests with toilet paper, a plunger and Airwick?

My recital moves on to the poem about Supta in the perfumed garden. A few people have left to assist the old man but I'm holding what's left of my audience in suspense with the suggestion of a sexual congress.

"You're missing the good parts," one man calls to the departed. Finally, the noise and confusion in the next room floods ours. I stand at the podium, my hands at my side.

"I thought someone shit a kitten. Do you smell that? We're lucky it didn't break the mirror. Who was last in there?' Dave Craddock is conducting the investigation.

All eyes turn to where I was standing.

"He used his poems to clean up. Where's the toilet paper?"
"Can you get that thing to flush?

"Not without a plunger."

I'm out the back porch and circling the edge of the parking lot. I'm wearing Totes, shorts, a red sports jacket over a Jet sweatshirt and a beret. It's my escape ensemble. I can hear the Rotarians inside.

I walk heel to toe like I'm taking a sobriety test across the parking lot as a car pulls in. The door opens and Gordon gets out. Turns out that Gordon is the guest speaker I opened for. He hugs me and we go back inside, Dave Craddock gives him a great big bear hug. Gordon walks around shaking hands with every club member. No one says anything to me about the bathroom. With everybody in their seats, Gordon begins his remarks. My poems have served their purpose.

"God culminates in the present. If we don't find him here, we will not find him anywhere." Gordon opens with a transcendental slogan. "Gentlemen, we are charged with preserving the nobility we possess. Thoreau is our greatest philosopher, the Father of the transcendental movement in America. We are sitting on sacred ground. Hometowns of other famous Americans boast libraries and monuments. We have not done justice to this man who lived among us. Walden Pond is unkempt and under-marketed." Gordon controls the scold in his voice but we all feel as if we've peed on the grave of a saint.

"Rotarians are held to a higher standard. The town of Concord can't do it alone. Every Rotary Club in the state needs to kick in. Let's not lose wisdom that should be shared with our grandchildren. It may take a dozen generations before we see the likes of him again. Are we men, if we don't act like men?"

I sit off to the side of the podium, looking at the floor. I pray that Gordon goes on for hours. When I make accidental eye contact with a man in the back of the room, he holds his nose with two fingers. Everyone is listening to Gordon out of respect. My crime is on the shelf for the time being. The poems I left in the can were some of my best.

Gordon produces a flip chart and a rendering of a single-room retreat house based on Thoreau's cabin. He proposes to erect thirty of these units around Walden Pond as a living memorial to his Guru. The public can rent them out like campsites at a State Park. The revenue from rentals will be used to preserve the pond and surrounding woods. The units are for individual retreats only, no guests and no parties. Park Rangers will enforce these rules.

"My aim is to create the Walden experience for a new generation and a generation after that. I want everyone here to write to their local legislatures urging them to pass the Walden bill. In return I will continue to crisscross this state enlisting support from interested parties." Gordon makes it sound as if a deal has been made. He carefully closes the flip cart, faces the audience, takes off his glasses, and rubs his eyes, puts his glasses back on and leans forward on the podium.- the same moves he used in India. He begins his closing remarks.

"Man's problems arise from his inability to sit alone in a room. I'm quoting Blasé Pascal and suggesting we need to give people a chance to try. Not today, not tomorrow but at sometime in the future the efforts we have made here today will enable the State of Massachusetts to rise to a more perfect day. Gentlemen thank you and God bless you." Straight out of the Hindu dinner circuit, Gordon's game is unchanged. There's a flare of applause and then Dave stands to encourage more. He waves a black sombrero.

"Gordon is doing the Lord's work. I know he won't like this but I have to add that he does it at his own expense. Why don't we send the hat around and see if we can't collect a bowl of lucky bucks to help with gas and tolls. Young man will you do the honors?" He hands the hat to me and takes Gordon to the bar. I start to circle in a hostile crowd.

"Here you go, Loadmaster." The first man throws a five.

"Wipe your ass with this." Another throws a wad of singles as he accidentally kicks me in the shins.

"A regular Robert Frostbite, dumpy boy." A ten spot accompanies an elbow to the ribs.

"Left us quite a pickle, didn't you Dudley?" Cigar smoke is blown in my face.

No one gives with any real enthusiasm. The bucks are "lucky" because good luck comes to a giver – this myth is a founding principle in Rotary fund-raising.

"Your poems suck and you trashed our bathroom." With the next contribution a lit cigarette touches the back of my hand and I drop the hat. Down on my knees, I have to pick the money up as the group mills around me. I go out to the bar and join Gordon and our host. "So you two know each other. What are the odds of that happening?" Dave wants to know.

In Gordon's car, I count the money,

"You made two hundred and ten dollars in twenty minutes."

"What are you doing here and what did you do back there to piss off those people?"

"I was reciting my poems about India."

"You brought them?"

"I covered for you."

"Do you want to stop and get something to eat? I missed lunch."

At the Carlisle Café, I lay my cards on the lunch counter. It's been twenty years since I ate with Gordon. He's retired from college and taken up a Thoreau crusade. I go into exacting detail about Surrinder, Shiva, the linga, and the funny clothes I'm wearing. I drink coffee with no effect. My purge at the Rotary was so complete if I swallowed two coins they would rattle.

"What can I do?"

"Take me to get the linga. I don't have a dime until I hand that thing off"

"I have an appointment tomorrow."

Gordon pays the tab.

"I apologize for insisting but I have no one else to turn to Gordo. It must be divine intervention, us meeting like this. I would call it unbelievable but after this weekend I've raised the bar on unbelievable."

"Shall we make a move?" Gordon rises.

"That's what I want to hear from my India captain."

"Please."

In the parking lot of the police station, I see my car parked next to a flatbed. I look in the window. The linga is gone. Inside the station, the desk Sergeant suggests the Captain will be in a better mood if we let him finish his dinner.

"You're the fella set fire to Thoreau's place?" He's erasing an answer in a crossword.

"Built a fire, not set a fire. It was that or freeze to death." I'm looking at the cop, then Gordon, then back.

"That's State Park property."

"So I've heard." My eyebrows are doing jumping jacks.

"Does the Sheriff know we're waiting?" I ask.

"He will when I tell him."

I flop in the seat next to Gordon. "Do you ever think about our time in India?"

"Not really."

"Do you ever hear from any of the guys?"

"No, how about you?"

"I thought I saw Randy in a supermarket but I was already in line."

The Sheriff opens the door and invites us in his office. There are Chinese food containers in a wastebasket under the window. He talks directly to Gordon.

"Your friend here is in a world of shit. I caught him camping at a State Historical site. The campfire is going to cost him $250 if it's a first offense. He can't provide ownership papers on the vehicle he was driving and we think we found stolen goods inside it. He hasn't produced a driver's license; that vehicle doesn't move until he does. I don't know if you know what went on at the Rotary lunch but I'm getting calls from people telling me to put my foot up this kid's ass. So what can I do for you?"

"How was dinner?" Gordon asks. I slump in my chair.

"That General Tso made some good chicken."

"That's why the other guy is only a Colonel."

"I get it," the Sheriff smiles.

As a salesman, I'm in awe as Gordon waltzes this Mayberry lawman around with small talk. He asks about the diplomas on the wall. Twenty minutes later, the sheriff is laying out a pass pattern he ran in a high school championship. Then he's dragging out family photos from a desk drawer. They haven't said a word about me. In disbelief, I watch Gordon move as Ali. He's taken my jailer from comedy to drama. He's talking about the son the Sheriff lost in Nam.

"I know your son's outfit from Pinksville, spring of '68. They were a bunch of good old boys, every one of them." Gordon snaps a salute at a photo of a young Marine.

With no notice of me, the two men embrace. I feel like the fat kid at a prom watching his friends dance. The Sheriff insists on a toast to American war dead. Drawing a bottle from the bottom of his desk, he sets out two glasses - do the math. By six o'clock the two have put a dent in a bottle. The Sheriff insists on taking Gordon home to meet his wife. I'm shown to a cell where I'm to spend the night. This is to placate the Rotary more than anything else. I see the linga still strapped to my luggage cart in the cell next to mine.

"Can I use the men's room first?" I ask.

"Hell no!"

Gordon gives me the same look he used when I stood to read my poetry at our India dinners.

a fat man under a beach umbrella

points a cigar at the Indian Ocean

his wife sunbathes naked

tanning the body of a girl half her age

Goa is a Portuguese pearl

in the fold of India's loin cloth

rookeries of bare ass Europeans

lie on a beach white as wall paint

an American with an Etch A Sketch

dares a sketch of the Fraulein

but she rolls on her tummy

her shape apes the breaking waves

the breeze is a kiss of pan

a Sikh at the surf flies an orange kite

it climbs a ladder to the royal blue sky

escapes through the roof of the world

Lock down at the Carlisle jail starts when the Sheriff leaves me in the charge of an underling. As soon as the cell door clangs closed, I grip the bars and recall the poems I wrote in college--yarns about the great and lonely lives of infamous cons. One told of two brothers who used their cell as a lending library. The inmates dubbed them Barnes and Noble. A little known vignette about Bob Stroud followed by the antics of Carl Panzaram, Gary Gilmore and the fevered sleep of Al Capone. I pace my windowless cell recalling lines. It's my second poetry recital of the day.

I have a cot and a table with a Bible on it. There's no sink or toilet. This is nothing more than a drunk tank. It holds no hope for rehabilitation. Inside the cover of the Bible, someone has written, "Error is an inn on the road to perfection."

I shut the Bible and lie down on the cot. I'm still wearing my Rotary blazer. I don't remember Gordon ever mentioning he was in Vietnam. Perhaps I should have paid closer attention to him. He was the salesman I wish I was today. The way he turned the Sheriff was ballet.

I close my eyes and consider my circumstance. After a nap so short I'm uncertain I slept, I'm back pacing the cell. If I wait until morning, I can walk out of here having paid my debt to society. A whole different matter will be getting the linga to Shiva. I'm late and I recall him saying he had little time. How does a Hindu God run short on time? The snowstorm makes for an easy excuse. Another taste of the flaming third eye must be avoided. I decide I don't have a minute to waste stirring in this cooler. The artist is a man of action. Guess who said that?

Through the door to the outer office, I can hear Monday Night Football – Bears vs. Patriots. There are the raised voices of the announcers over a cheering crowd. In the cell next to me, the linga lies, indifferent to sports.

I sit back down and await inspiration. It comes in the aroma of delivered pizza. The underling comes in to offer me two slices. I ask him the score of the game.

"No score, halfway through the first quarter."

"How long have you been a Pats fan?" I'm thinking of Gordon wooing the Sheriff.

"Are you writing a book?" He turns his back to me. "No, you can't watch the game; Jet boy." My choice of sweatshirt is a serious mistake. In sales, avoid self-created obstacles.

When he leaves, he doesn't lock my cell. I'm pissed that my overture to Barney was rebuffed. As a sales professional I should have played that kid smooth as a one hop to a shortstop. I'm going to make him the laughing stock of Carlisle law enforcement.

I button the red blazer around my pillow in homage to Frank White and his break from Alcatraz. The Bible inside my pillow case represents my head. While throwing a sheet over the form, I hear my keeper yelling at the TV.

From the adjoining cell, I roll the linga out -.careful not to make a sound. I can hear his chair creaking and the burp of a pop top through the door. Awaiting opportunity, I whisper prison verses to myself. I stiffen when I hear him get up and walk to where I remember seeing the bathroom. In a feat of New England modesty, he closes the door behind him. The first thing I see as I ease into the outer office is my car keys hanging on a hook by the door. I pick them off the hook and put them in my mouth. An orange key fob hangs down on my chin like a hipster goatee. My pizza-sharing warden must be enjoying an evacuation as dramatic as the one I authored at the Rotary Club. Out the door like Tom Thumb, stole a pig and away he run, I go to my car. If the deputy in the bathroom doesn't take anything more than a quick glimpse at my cell, I'll be out of Concord before my escape is uncovered.

The parking lot slopes toward the street so I let the car roll backward. I start the engine when the car stops. A block away I turn the radio up and sing along with Elton John. At a red light I head bump the linga sitting in the passenger seat like a mutant peanut MM. I'm breathing free man air.

At the kitchen table of Lord Shiva, I await a break in his mediation. He's currently off-line. On the table is a police report covering the theft of stones from his home. Everything I brought up the other day is gone. My linga sits on a kitchen chair between us. Shiva's pure white shawl throws its arm across his shoulder. I found him with such ease after my escape, I'm sure I was drawn here by his divine finger. His third eye is covered with a red dot suggesting the point at which you spot a cue ball.

"What happened to you?" Shiva returns to the moment.

"I wouldn't know where to start."

"Good, I have no time for cheap sales stories."

"Who stole your stones? Your wife?"

"I ask the questions."

"She doesn't want you over here in America. Your dharma is to be a God in India, not in Massachusetts. You're not to be trusted around all these willing American girls. You're a snake, a hound, a defiler of your marriage vows."

"Look who's talking."

"I confess to my own God. Keep me out of your marital problems."

"Your ignorance is divine."

"You need a linga to get laid, that's why your wife is so hot to keep them away from you."

"I can understand why you are so often fired."

"This is a curse placed on you by other Gods? You can't get yoni without linga?"

"I have no time for your jokes."

I slept with your wife while I was in Bayside. I thought I was having sex with Surrinder's wife but it couldn't have been her. I was tumbled by a Goddess."

"No, my wife slept with you and you would have never got back here if she wasn't sure you'd brag about it. She steals with one hand and gives with the other. It's her way of demonstrating her power of me."

"You sound a touch mortal."

"Careful with your words, I have no need of you now."

"She was hot." Without thinking, I adjust myself.

With a flick of a pop top he peels back his forehead dot and a beam of light sends me flying backwards across the floor till my head hits the stove. There's a difference between a dash, a hyphen, and a straight arm but in all cases two things are kept apart. I remind myself not to be familiar with divinity.

"I'm sorry."

"Now you're sorry?"

"Can I just get paid and go?"

"Of course."

"I lost those half hundreds you stuck me with."

"I'm sure my wife has them. You haven't been out of her sight since you left Bayside. She can pay her own errand boy."

"What are you going to do if she comes here?'

"Distance is the only antidote to her seductive powers. I'm heading to the west coast and the parishes consumed with phallic worship."

"San Francisco can be hilly."

"Her followers worship her yoni. Do you understand how fanatic they can be?"

"I know, believe me, I know."

I watch Shiva wipe his hand across the linga. Its sits on the chair between us like a favored child.

"I'm unlikely to get financial help from your wife. Could you just pay me what you promised plus a little extra to cover the expense of the second trip?

"You were conspiring to steal from me and now you ask me this?"

"Let's have a win/win. If I gave Surrinder, say, an additional thousand dollars he might forgive me for kidnapping the rock."

"It was mine from the minute he took my money."

"I doubt he'll see it that way."

"He was stealing it from me and using you to lie to me. The other stones you brought me have been stolen. Has everyone forgotten what a short-tempered God of Destruction I am?"

"What do you care about money?"

"Nothing."

"Then help me and I'm outta here."

"You're outta here anyway."

"Surrinder is not going to believe me if I say I didn't get paid."

"You're a salesman; make him believe."

"But I was working for you."

"I'm not your God."

"You're my employer."

"You're fried."

"Where have I heard this before?"

I fold up Shiva's couch. Overnight snow flurries adhere to the sticker residue on my car window. I ease out of Concord without looking back. There are a number of ways to kill time on a long drive. Make a list of all the Thoreau quotes you can think of. Recall long abandoned poems. Count up the women you've had and almost had. I've done all of these things on my first three drives. On the fourth and final ride, I have more than enough things to consider. I'm confronting a buffet table with a tea saucer.

I'm going to tell Surrinder I had no choice but to hijack the rock. I'll apologize for thinking I was sleeping with his wife when I was in the arms of a Hindu Goddess set on cuckolding her husband with an errand boy. I managed to squeeze one hundred dollars out of Shiva before we turned in last night. There is no job for me to go to when I get home and my daughter is scheduled to start karate. The car is trashed and getting towed off that hillside has done something to my transmission. There's a seven-second delay between shift and engage. I'm wearing Totes in an ill-heated vehicle with obscured windows. I'm not whistling Dixie but I haven't quit either. In sales, problems are opportunities in work clothes. I'm recalling the conversation between Shiva and me after he fired me. He offered me his sofa bed if I swore to leave in the morning without a farewell.

"There is no sense in leaving without money for gas and tolls."

He opens a coffee can and hands me a hundred.

"I appreciate this but it hardly covers my costs." A good salesman knows no reverse.

"Didn't you just explain to me that I'm harboring an escaped prisoner who the Sheriff is certain stole this stone from me? You're saying I haven't done enough for you?"

In sales be careful what you tell people about yourself. It can backfire. Disguise your needs and desires. Make others talk; avoid accounts of your own. If there is anything to be learned from your past, you should know it already. Reveal nothing without knowing a purpose for

216

revealing it. Live by the Arab proverb "Hide what you know, what you own, and the road you intend to travel."

I'm traveling on I-95 for the fourth time since I cracked that wishbone at my sister's Thanksgiving. If I wished for riches I've whiffed. I replay my attempt at putting Shiva on a guilt trip.

"I'm screwed. You think you have a pissed off wife? I've got a stack of bills and nothing to show for it. I did all this as a favor for Surrinder. A show of loyalty and love for India was all I was thinking. I never meant to hurt you."

"You're pathetic, go to bed."

"Give me a couple of hundred more and I'll never write another poem about India."

"You would do that?

Getting more is the first thing on the menu of a veteran rep. Once their wallet is open, keep it that way. Shiva has already given me a hundred, why not a hundred more? The trick is to keep talking. I want to be paid to shut up

"My uncle is a big shot on Wall Street - corner office, 25th floor, private bathroom. He takes his five and seven year old daughters to work to show off how important he is. The girls go through the revolving door into the lobby. They insist on going around again and around again while Daddy holds their coats. When they get home, the revolving door is all they talk about. My uncle realizes he didn't change the way his daughters thought about him but they changed the way he thought about that door."

"Why are you telling me this?" Shiva asks.

"Look, there's only so much we're prepared to appreciate. So many sublime and erotic things have happened to me since I undertook this linga delivery. Yet I have to focus on the unglamorous commodity of cash. Not for my own indulgence but for those of my loved ones."

"Shut up and go to bed."

"A closed mouth does not get fed, my Lordship. I have to ask."

"You've asked, the answer is no."

Shiva winds up giving me the four other half hundreds. Their brothers were lost in a war that made no sense. I announce to no one that the very last thing I'll ever consider is a drive back to Carlisle. I'd rather read Walden while standing on one foot.

Bored to tears, I'm scanning AM radio talk shows. I recognize Gordon's voice on a Boston station. He's doing a pitch for the "Walden Reclamation Project". Don't bet against him getting what he wants. There's a difference between envy, jealousy, and grudging respect, I'm guilty of all three. If I could sell with the art of Gordon, I wouldn't be humbled by the chore of funding karate.

"How the hell could I make a living writing poetry?" I'm screaming at my radio like a mental patient.

"Just begin." I hear Gordon breathe into the microphone.

our desert trek leader

Mister Jimmy Singh Deo

suggests a party of six to the Thar

to walk a dead riverbed

home to a lost civilization

in his sitting room at Bhubaneswar

his wife Baby aglow with child

serves tea and charm

as he dares us on a map

to walk across the face of time

"In a twenty thousand year old desert

a man finds himself in humbling company

tribes have crossed this wasteland

since fire was a slip in the suggestion box

no nation pretends ownership

on a road tour of waterholes

the wild ass of Rann

race across salt flats

chased by the memory of predators

whose bones crunch beneath our boots

our shadows stretch over dune crests

the soundtrack is our breathing

God whispers in Hindi

we are in the world of sand

tracking armies of ancient kings

the clink of a cowbell carries

across miles of silence

and things said back home

put on grander robes

in a world of new meanings

There's a parking space in front of the brick Monopoly house that sits atop my basement apartment. That only happens in the movies. I hope it's an omen. At the side door I find a FED EX package. Inside is my wallet with the four half hundreds and some of my stolen clothes.

"I had sneakers," I whisper under my breath.

Downstairs, my dump never looked so chic. I marvel at the painted wall paneling and a niche filled with Argo corn starch boxes. Playing "Better Things" by the Kinks, I dance as a mental patient. My bed waits like a blushing bride.

I plan to troll airport diners looking for an owner who thinks a salesman is the answer to his company's flat line. That myth has put food on my table for years. It's not Whole Foods but it is good food. Karate is covered but everything else is yet to be paid. If I owe you money, you'll see it in a couple of weeks.

www.ingramcontent.com/pod-product-compliance
Lightning Source LLC
Chambersburg PA
CBHW071333250626
47159CB00004B/1588